GENTLE PERSUASION

Considering the hostility she had felt towards Anton Van der Buren at their first meeting, Lorna was surprised at how much and how soon her feelings towards him had changed. But Anton was going to have to do a lot of persuading if he expected their relationship to develop into anything deeper than friendship . . .

GENTLE PERSUASION

BY

CLAUDIA JAMESON

MILLS & BOON LIMITED
15–16 BROOK'S MEWS
LONDON W1A 1DR

First published 1983
Australian copyright 1983
Philippine copyright 1983
This edition 1983

© Claudia Jameson 1983

ISBN 0 263 74397 7

Set in Monophoto Times 10 on 10½ pt.
01–1183 – 59910

Made and printed in Great Britain by
Richard Clay (The Chaucer Press) Ltd,
Bungay, Suffolk

CHAPTER ONE

THE magazine was there, lying with the morning paper on the floor behind the door of her shop. As she bent to pick them up, the postman pushed several envelopes through the door and gave her a friendly wave as he passed the shop window.

Lorna Stewart instinctively pulled her dressing-gown closer around herself. There was something about the postman that reminded her of Jake Dougan, and she shuddered at the thought. She did not normally think about the distant past, she had trained herself not to, but it was there, making its contribution to the person she was today. And it would always be there. Fortunately she was satisfied, now, with the person she had become and she had reached the stage where she could put the past, all of it, well and truly behind her. She returned the postman's wave and picked up the envelopes.

Normally she did not venture downstairs until she was fully dressed and made up, until her image reflected precisely what she was—the well-groomed, smartly-dressed owner of *Feline*, one of the nicest ladieswear shops in Windsor. Well, that was how she liked to think of it, anyway. True, the shop was small, but it was filled with carefully selected, expensive garments which spoke of quality and good taste. It *was* one of the nicest ladieswear shops in Windsor. In just less than a year *Feline* had established a good reputation among its discerning customers. Lorna Stewart gave good service, honest guidance and she took pains to see that her customers got what they wanted. For this, they were perfectly happy to pay, and Lorna catered for the type of woman who was perfectly able to pay.

This morning, however, she did not take time to look

5

proudly around the shop as she normally did on first stepping into it. This morning, she was going to take pride in Cathy's achievements instead of her own. Lorna hugged the magazine against her breast and went back upstairs to the flat above the shop. Like Lorna, her half-sister had worked very hard to get herself established and she deserved the success which was just starting to become hers.

Lorna had seen little of Cathy during the past few months, owing to the fact that they were both so busy in their own ways, but they chatted frequently on the telephone and kept up to date with the news. On the odd occasions when Lorna had expressed concern over her half-sister's current lifestyle, Cathy had laughed it off, reminding her that she was more than capable of looking after herself. She was, of course. Cathy was only nineteen, but she had been brought up the hard way—they had both grown up the hard way. The need for success, the instinct for survival, was just as strong in Cathy as it was in Lorna.

No, she ought not to worry about Cathy. But she did. Maybe it was just a habit. She had always worried over the younger girl and no doubt she always would. She had always protected Cathy fiercely, to the best of her ability, but the girl was not unscathed by life.

Lorna smiled at that thought as she opened the magazine and found the pages she was looking for. There was Cathy among several other girls who were modelling a range of evening dresses for autumn/winter. On the next page, occupying the entire page, Cathy stood alone wearing a black cocktail-length dress with her blonde hair piled high on the crown of her head and her lovely face reflecting nothing but happiness. She certainly looked untouched by life, and she looked beautiful.

Lowering herself into the armchair near the gas fire, Lorna poured herself a cup of tea and continued to look at the photographs. They had been taken for the magazine weeks ago, in preparation for this special edition featuring ladieswear for autumn, and Cathy had been thrilled about the assignment. Printed vertically alongside the pictures was the photographer's name, Van der Buren. There was no forename, just Van der Buren. Lorna read the accompanying copy, then put the magazine down with a smile. Models, photographer and copywriter had done a damn good job. So Cathy had got herself into a glossy magazine! In time she would make the front cover, no doubt. She certainly had the face and figure for it.

People had often remarked how alike the two girls were, though Lorna couldn't see it. She was fairly tall, but Cathy was taller; she was slim, but Cathy was slimmer, and whereas Cathy had long blonde hair, Lorna's was short and auburn, distinctly coppery with very attractive natural highlights.

By nine-thirty, Lorna was dressed and putting the finishing touches to her make-up. Facially, she and Cathy were a little alike, especially around the eyes. They had both inherited the positive green eyes of their mother. But that was really where the resemblance ended, in Lorna's opinion ... except for one other thing. They were both attractive to men, very much so, and while Cathy revelled in that fact, Lorna found it a constant irritation. Lorna wasn't interested. As far as their attitudes to men were concerned, and in their personalities, the two half-sisters could not be more different.

Dressed in a dark green, fine wool dress which had been expensive even at cost price, Lorna surveyed herself in the full-length mirror. The addition of a toning silk scarf, tucked into the vee neckline of the dress, made the outfit complete. She stepped into a pair of black patent leather shoes and nodded in satisfaction. There were days when her mood was such that she didn't feel like dressing so smartly and making up, but she did it because she had to look the part. In a way, she was an advertisement for her own shop, wasn't she? She had an image to maintain. Besides, she could always relax totally on Sundays, when *Feline* was closed.

'Ooh, it's rather nippy today!' Lorna's assistant, Dulcie, came through the door at five minutes to ten, as usual. She shivered as she stepped into the warmth of the shop and went straight to the stock room at the back and put the kettle on for coffee. 'Let's hope the cold doesn't scare off what's left of the tourists!'

'I'll second that!' Lorna called cheerfully. She was making a note of the situation as far as her stock of tights was concerned. She stocked only two of the most expensive brands of stockings and tights and these were bought mainly on impulse, though sometimes customers would ask for a pair specifically to see what a dress looked like when it was worn with the right shade of tights.

Items such as these, and scarves and belts and so on, made only a small contribution to Lorna's takings, but they occupied a negligible amount of space, and she had found from experience that sometimes the addition of a small accessory could clinch the sale of an expensive garment. And Lorna was not one to lose a sale!

She put down her notepad, turned the sign on the door to 'open' and joined Dulcie in the stockroom. 'How was your weekend?'

It was Thursday today, in fact, but since Dulcie only worked Thursdays and Fridays the question was not unusual, because they hadn't seen each other since the weekend. Lorna had two other assistants on Saturdays, one of whom was a student and the other of whom worked the first half of the week, too. Of the three she much preferred Dulcie, who was forty, affluent and working part-time, not because she needed the money but because she needed something to occupy her time.

'Super. We went out to dinner on Saturday and had a houseful of visitors on Sunday. And you?' She smiled at Lorna, knowing more or less what her answer would be.

Lorna smiled and nodded, not bothering to answer

because she had spent her weekend the way she spent most of her weekends. On Saturday nights she went through the entire stock of the shop and did her books, and on Sundays, if she ventured out at all, it was only as far as a local restaurant or perhaps for a walk. From time to time she would go to a concert or the theatre, in London or at Windsor's Theatre Royal, but that was generally to give herself a break mid-week.

Lorna loved Windsor, so full of character and history and, during the season, its tourists from all the corners of the globe. She had seen everything there was to see in the town during the year she'd lived there, and she knew almost everything there was to know about the place. Some of the local residents resented the influx of tourists, but to Lorna they meant sales and sales meant profit.

'I know this shop means everything to you,' Dulcie said cautiously, 'but you don't seem to have much of a life apart from it, Lorna. I mean——'

The tinkling of the bell on the outer door of the shop brought Dulcie to her feet and Lorna let her go and see to the customer. Duleie was reliable and trustworthy and as good a saleswoman as Lorna in her own, tactful way. And that meant she was very good.

Sipping at her coffee, Lorna made a conscious effort to quell the slight irritation Dulcie's last words provoked in her. She was well aware that Dulcie found her something of a mystery. So did everyone else to a greater or lesser extent. Nobody but Cathy really understood Lorna, nobody but she knew what motivated her, what angered her, frightened her or pleased her.

But that was the way Lorna wanted things to be. She wasn't in the habit of talking about herself and she certainly was not in the habit of talking about her background. She knew what her assistant was thinking, what she had been about to say, and it was true. For a young woman of twenty-five, Lorna lived a very quiet life. Her entire world revolved around her business. Oh, she was friendly enough. With her staff she was friendly, if a little demanding; she expected a fair day's work for a fair day's pay. With her customers she was charming but honest, and other people, her acquaintances, found her quite warm.

But Lorna's friendliness only went so far. She saw no reason, no need, to talk about her private self. What need was there to tell people how she had slaved to get out of the poverty trap? What reason was there to tell people she had vowed fervently that she would never, ever, be ill-treated again?

Certainly she lived a quiet life apart from the shop. She did so by choice. For almost a year, for the first time in her life, she had known what it was to have peace. For the first time in her life, she was happy.

When the bell tinkled for the second time, Lorna shook herself mentally and sprang to her feet. She went into the shop to find Eve Summers standing there, looking like the cat that had got the cream. 'Well! You're looking pleased with yourself!'

'Good morning, Lorna!' Eve giggled almost girlishly. 'I've got news. Boy, have I got news!' She glanced towards Dulcie and the customer she was serving, then quickly back to Lorna. 'Any chance of you popping out for coffee? I'll only keep you fifteen minutes or so.'

'Try and stop me,' Lorna smiled. It didn't occur to her to tell Eve that she'd just had a cup of coffee. Eve was a customer, a regular, all-year-round customer who spent freely. She was twenty-nine, she was a little trendy in an expensive sort of way and she bought nearly all her clothes from Lorna. On her buying trips in London, Lorna often picked up items specifically with Eve in mind. She understood the other woman's taste very well and had given up trying to influence her as to what really suited her. The truth was that Eve often bought clothes which didn't flatter her in the least, but her individuality, or perhaps stubbornness, was such that she would rarely accept Lorna's guidance.

The two of them got on very well and occasionally

had lunch together. Eve was a solicitor, a well-spoken, well-educated woman who had obviously been brought up with money. The offices where she worked were in Park Street, just a short walk from *Feline*, and Eve had handled the legalities of the lease on Lorna's shop when she first took over. And she had been her best customer ever since.

'Do I need my coat?' Lorna asked, curious to hear the news and knowing it must be something big which had taken Eve away from her work.

'In a word, yes. I think winter's arrived.'

'Don't say that—it's only October, for heaven's sake! It's *autumn*.'

'Autumn, October—whatever. The fact is, it's freezing out there.' Eve's ready laughter was infectious, and Lorna grinned at her.

'Give me a moment and I'll be right with you.'

They walked briskly to the Castle Hotel coffee shop and gave their order to the waitress. Across the road was Windsor Castle, old, proud and resplendent in its dominant position overlooking the town. Familiar though it was, the sight of it never failed to please Lorna, but right now her attention was focused on Eve.

'I'm waiting,' she said with mock impatience.

'You haven't guessed?' Eve teased. 'Surely you've guessed!'

'I haven't got the first clue,' Lorna said honestly. She could not imagine what had happened that was making Eve look so happy, almost glowing, even.

'Julian's proposed!' The words came out in a rush and then she repeated them, looking at Lorna expectantly.

Taken aback, Lorna had to make an effort to give the required response. She smiled warmly and gave her congratulations, but she couldn't hold back her questions and her surprise was genuine. 'But—but you've always told me you weren't interested in marriage! I mean, your career—you've always said that your career——'

'I love my career,' Eve nodded vigorously. 'But I love Julian more. Besides, I can have both, can't I?'

'I suppose so. It's just——'

'I know, I know.' Eve held up a hand. 'I've always gone on about my freedom. I'm happy in my work, I adore my little house, but for a long time now I'd had the feeling that something was missing in my life. You're on your own, Lorna. The only family you have is your sister, isn't it? Don't you ever feel there's something missing in your life?'

'No,' Lorna said simply.

'A man, for example?'

'No.' Inwardly, Lorna smiled. She had said the word very mildly, too much in control of herself to blurt out to Eve that a man was the last thing in life she was looking for.

Eve shrugged. 'As soon as Julian joined the practice, I knew what was missing in my life. I think I started falling in love with him straight away. If I'm honest, I'll admit that I've been hoping for the past three months that he'd ask me to marry him.'

Eve and Julian had been going out for the past six months, just less than the time he had been a partner in the practice. Lorna had met him several times when he had come into the shop with Eve, and he seemed pleasant enough. 'So it's going to be a family of solicitors, is it?' she smiled. 'Where will you live? In Julian's flat or in your house?'

'Neither. We'll buy something bigger. Not too far away, of course.'

And is he quite happy for you to go on working?'

'I haven't got round to asking him that!' Eve reached up to tuck her hair behind her ears. It was light brown and very straight and she took not the slightest trouble over it. She just let it hang to her shoulders and tucked it behind her ears when it got in the way. 'I've had a good run,' she went on, laughing. 'I'm almost thirty. I've had my fun. I'm ready to settle down.'

'I suppose so.' Lorna wasn't going to comment further. This was, after all, none of her business, and if Eve was happy then Lorna was pleased for her. It was just that the news had been unexpected; Lorna hadn't realised how serious things had been between the couple. She signalled the waitress for the bill just as Eve glanced at her watch.

'Yes, I can't linger,' Eve said. 'I've got a client coming at eleven, and I promised you I wouldn't keep you long.' She took the bill from the waitress before Lorna had a chance to.

'Well, hang on a minute, Eve! You haven't told me when the big day is.'

'We haven't named it yet. Give us a chance! This only happened last night, you know. We'll have to confer with both our families, I'm afraid.'

'Have they been told?'

'Yes, we've done that much. And we've decided to make the engagement official on my birthday.'

'Oh!' Again, Lorna was surprised. This struck her as being very formal—an unofficial, then an official engagement, the need to confer with both families over the marriage.

'Don't worry, the party's still on. Doubly so! Now, it'll be a birthday-cum-engagement party. You have kept the date free, haven't you?'

'Of course,' Lorna said kindly. A couple of weeks ago Eve had mentioned that she would be having a birthday party in December and had invited Lorna. Lorna had accepted, but she was having trouble, now, trying to remember the precise date. She did not, of course, need to consult her diary to know that she'd be free that evening! 'It's on the twenty ... I'm afraid I can't remember.'

'The twenty-ninth,' Eve provided. 'Right in the middle of Christmas and New Year. But things have changed rather. I won't be giving the party at home, I'll be giving it at my parents' house. Or rather, they will! They live in Hampshire—I hope that won't put you out too much? I mean, you'll still come? You'll stay the night with us, of course.'

'Of course I'll come! I'll be quite happy to stay the night, if there's room.'

'Bags of it.' Eve got to her feet. 'The party will be much bigger than I anticipated, in the circumstances.' She put her hand on Lorna's arm as they left the coffee shop. 'Lorna, what are you doing over Christmas? Julian and I will be at my parents' house throughout Christmas and the New Year. Would you like to spend the holidays with us? I'd be so pleased if you could!'

Lorna was genuinely pleased by this, but she had to decline. 'That's sweet of you, and I'm grateful. But I'll be spending Christmas with my sister, Cathy. We always spend Christmas together.'

'Bring her with you!' Eve chatted on, buttoning her coat against the wind. 'It's open house at my parents' place, you know. They'd be delighted. They love having guests.'

Tactfully, Lorna declined. She couldn't envisage two total strangers being welcome in someone's house over Christmas, no matter how hospitable the hosts. Besides, she saw less and less of Cathy these days and the holidays would be a good opportunity for them to have a natter. She said goodbye to Eve at the corner of Peascod Street, declining the Christmas invitation but assuring her she would be at the engagement party.

Filled with a sense of well-being, Lorna walked back to the shop. Life was good, these days, really good. She had never doubted that she would get on in life; she had made up her mind on that at a very early age. It had been a long, hard slog against the odds for one with her background, but she had made it. And the rewards were great. She had not only her business but a cosy little flat in one of the prettiest parts of England. She mixed with nice people now, people like Dulcie and Eve, people who accepted her totally for what she had striven to become. Nothing had stood in her way, and neither Jake Dougan nor anything else had prevented her from keeping a balanced view on life. Considering the damage Jake Dougan had done to her, that in itself was quite an achievement.

'Don't tell me you've had a mad rush?' She stepped into the shop to find Dulcie surrounded by almost the entire stock of knitwear. 'Or was it a question of finding the right size in the right colour in the right style?'

'Something like that!' Dulcie looked pleased with herself as she slipped sweaters in their plastic bags back on to the shelves against a wall. 'But it was worth it. I've just sold eight—*eight* Pringle jumpers and three cardigans! How about that?'

'Great!' Lorna shrugged her coat off. 'Someone with a fetish for Scottish knitwear, I take it?'

'Two foreign ladies. Greek, I think. They didn't speak a word of English, but they knew exactly what they wanted. I suppose they were buying gifts to take home. A present from Britain, and all that!'

'How did they pay?' Lorna frowned. It was by no means unusual for tourists to make multiple purchases, but one had to exercise a certain amount of caution as far as cheques and credit cards were concerned.

'In cash, don't worry.' Dulcie was smiling at her now, rather than with her. She had privately reached the conclusion that Lorna's scepticism extended beyond her business dealings. 'Crisp ten-pound notes fresh from the bank—with all their watermarks in place!'

Lorna looked at her quickly. 'One can't be too careful, Dulcie. I've learnt that from experience.' She said it mildly enough, but Dulcie made no further attempt to tease her.

The morning continued pleasantly. A couple of people came in to browse but didn't buy. A young woman with two children came in to ask the price of a blouse, tried to hide her disappointment on being told this and left with the excuse that she would have to call back later to try it on. Neither Lorna nor Dulcie made any attempt to make a sale, because it was obvious that the woman didn't have enough money.

Just before lunchtime, a rep from one of the fashion houses came in and Lorna gave him a repeat order. Then, as she knew he would, he asked her to join him for lunch.

'Sorry, I've got too much to do, Paul. Thanks anyway.' Lorna smiled pleasantly at the good-looking young man who didn't seem to know how to keep business and pleasure separate. Shortly after opening the shop, Lorna had accepted an invitation from him because she had considered it business and nothing else. She was a customer; reps did this sort of thing from time to time, so she had thought nothing of it.

But Paul had asked her to dinner before their lunch was over and he had been far too familiar, far too *touchy*, when he had escorted her back to the shop. She had declined the invitation to dinner, of course.

'Persistent, isn't he?' Dulcie said lightly when Paul had gone. 'I suppose one has to admire that, really.'

'Some people just don't know how to take no for an answer,' Lorna shrugged. She was well aware that Dulcie realised how much the man fancied her—it was plain for anyone to see.

'Not your type, I suppose?' Dulcie was probing for a response, but there was none forthcoming. She liked Lorna, but she couldn't weigh her up. She wondered what type of man Lorna *would* be interested in. Still, she let the subject drop. Lorna was the boss, after all, and she was perfectly entitled to keep herself to herself.

Dulcie popped out to buy their sandwiches then, and no sooner had she closed the door behind her than the telephone rang. The extension of Lorna's upstairs telephone was in the stockroom and she hurried to answer it, not dreaming that her day, her routine, her inner peace was about to be destroyed by the call.

'It's Cathy.' Her sister's voice sounded strained, pitched higher than normal. 'Are you going buying today? Are you coming into London?'

Lorna's hand tightened on the telephone receiver.

'Well—no. I went buying yesterday. Is . . . is something wrong, Cathy?'

There was a long silence and then a muffled sound as Cathy started sobbing. She was crying so hard that she couldn't speak, and Lorna became frantic. 'What is it? Cathy! Cathy? Tell me, please! What's wrong?'

Cathy told her nothing, she just sobbed. It was so unlike her, so very unlike Cathy to cry—let alone carry on like this. 'Cathy, listen. I'll be right over. Stay where you are, I'll be there as quickly as I can.'

'No. It's——' Cathy managed to get a couple of words out, but Lorna had already put the phone down. She dashed upstairs for her car keys, flung her coat on then stood waiting impatiently for Dulcie to come back.

She composed herself as she waited, but inwardly she felt frightened, upset. It was so unlike Cathy to cry . . .

'Dulcie, I have to go into London.' Lorna spoke calmly as her assistant came in with their lunch, appearing not to notice the other woman's look of surprise.

'Anything wrong? I mean, you went buying yesterday, didn't you?'

Lorna's brief nod could have meant anything. 'Have you got your keys with you? Good. I'll probably be back before we close, but just in case—you'll lock up for me, Dulcie?'

'Of course.' Dulcie asked nothing further. 'See you tomorrow if I don't see you later.'

The traffic into London was heavy and got heavier as Lorna drove closer to the heart of the city. It took more than an hour for her to get to Holland Park, where Cathy had a flat, and a further twenty minutes for her to find a parking place.

Cathy was dry-eyed when she opened her door to her sister. Her eyes were puffy and there was something in her face, something about her attitude that Lorna had never seen in her before.

Lorna did not waste words. 'What is it, love?' she asked gently, hugging her sister protectively.

'I'll make some coffee.' Cathy stepped away from her, her tall, slender figure looking slimmer than ever as she walked into the kitchen.

Lorna glanced around as she followed her sister. Cathy's flat was as untidy as ever. On the floor were several pairs of expensive shoes which had been kicked off and left where they fell. Occupying an armchair was a new addition to her collection of stuffed toys—an outsize rabbit. Cathy spent her money as if it grew on trees. The last time Lorna had been in her bedroom, she'd counted over thirty bottles of perfume on the dressing table, not to mention the expensive pieces of jewellery and enough make-up to last a lifetime. And her clothes! Well, Cathy had enough of those to stock Lorna's shop all over again.

But all this was Cathy's idea of luxury. She was a hoarder of *things*, and Lorna understood it only too well. Heaven knew that Cathy had gone short of things in her childhood; there had been no luxuries then.

Her eyebrows rose slightly as she noticed a new fox fur coat draped over the back of a chair. That must have cost a fortune!

It was not unusual, however, that Cathy's living room was in chaos. The kitchen wasn't quite as bad, but then Cathy rarely cooked for herself, if ever. 'You've lost weight, Cathy. I know models are supposed to be slim, but really——'

Cathy's laughter cut off the words. It was harsh, bitter. 'Have I? That's a scream, in the circumstances.' Again she laughed, and Lorna felt her stomach contract nervously.

'The circumstances?'

'I'm pregnant, Lorna. Don't look at me like that! I said I'm pregnant. I'm not dying!' She snatched up the coffee mugs and went into the living room.

Lorna stayed where she was for a moment. She leaned heavily against the sink, her heart feeling like a great stone in her chest. Her disappointment was enormous and—yes, she was shocked. This sort of thing happened every day, the world over ... but to Cathy? To her little sister?

She went into the living room and sat opposite Cathy, momentarily stuck for words. 'Cathy, you—you're nineteen years old——'

Tight-lipped, Cathy reached for a packet of cigarettes. 'So?' She lit up, inhaling the smoke deeply. 'Lorna, will you take that look off your face. Don't judge me! So I'm nineteen—did you think I was a virgin or something? We're not all like you, you know——'

Lorna's eyes closed involuntarily and Cathy's apology came at once. 'Lorna, I'm sorry. Oh, God, I'm so sorry! Forgive me, I didn't mean to say that. It's just—it's just that I've been in such a panic.'

'It's all right. Forget it.' Lorna spoke quietly. Never, ever, had Cathy been so unkind, but it didn't matter.

'I've had a pregnancy test. I phoned for the results today and was told the test was positive. I panicked. I phoned you. But that was over an hour ago and I've been thinking hard ever since. You needn't have dashed over here. I'm grateful,' she added quickly, 'but I tried to tell you not to make a special journey if you weren't coming buying today. I have to go out shortly. Besides, there's nothing you can do, is there? What I have to do is obvious.'

Lorna kept an impassive face, but inwardly she was very upset. 'Look, I'm not judging—you've got to believe that. Who am I to judge? I'm just surprised you allowed this to happen. I don't mean ... getting pregnant is what I mean. I thought you could look after yourself. You're not naïve, Cathy. Why the devil don't you take the pill or something?'

'I am on the pill! But I forgot to take it one night. I was drunk, you see, and I——'

'Drunk?'

'Now don't start lecturing me!' Cathy snapped. 'It wasn't altogether my fault. Karel had invited me to dinner at his place in Knightsbridge, and what with the wine and the brandy.... After dinner, we carried on drinking as we talked—anyhow, never mind that. The point is, I forgot to take my pill. I went to bed with Karel for several nights on the trot and . . . bingo!' She tried very hard to be casual, but it didn't come off. Cathy was not herself. There was a tightness, a bitterness in her face which Lorna had never seen before.

Doing her utmost to keep calm about the whole thing, Lorna asked, 'And what does he say about it? This—Karel? I take it you've phoned him and told him?'

'No. He wouldn't be in the least interested.'

'*What?* What's that supposed to mean? Is he married, is that it?'

'No.'

'Karel who? Who is he?'

Cathy put out her cigarette. 'It doesn't matter. Look, you'll have to go. I have to be at my agency at four o'clock.'

Lorna didn't move. She had known for some months about Cathy living it up in the evenings, doing all the discos and nightclubs. She had tried to warn her to be a little more moderate, pointing out that late nights, drinking and so on would take its toll on her looks, and Cathy's livelihood as a model depended on her looks.

She examined her sister closely now, without being obvious about it. Cathy was a lot thinner—she skipped too many meals—but she was beautiful. She was also vulnerable. Oh, she was no fool and she was not naïve, but she was still, obviously, vulnerable to mistakes. 'If he isn't married, why the secrecy?'

'I'm not being secretive,' Cathy shrugged. 'It's Karel Van der Buren, since you're interested.' She looked at Lorna with a mixture of defiance and expectation.

Lorna knew the name. She had seen it in print only a few hours earlier. 'The photographer.'

'The photographer. He's becoming really well known, you know. He's very good. Did you get the magazine today, by the way? Did you see the photographs?'

Lorna's nod was brief. 'What did you mean earlier, when you said what you had to do is obvious? You say Karel doesn't know about this yet, so——'

'Nor will he.' Cathy drained her coffee mug and picked up her cigarettes, lighting one before she spoke again. 'I'm going to have an abortion.'

'Cathy—Cathy wait a minute——'

'Don't interfere!' she snapped. 'It's my decision and I've made up my mind!'

'But——'

'But nothing!'

'Shut up and listen,' Lorna said firmly. 'You have to tell Karel. He might offer a different solution.' Cathy was still panicking. She might have thought herself over her shock, but she wasn't.

Cathy laughed hollowly. 'If you think he'd offer to marry me, you've got another think coming! He loves his freedom, he's a womaniser, he's arrogant and ambitious!'

Shocked, Lorna stared at her. 'If you know he's all these things, why did you——'

'Because he's also very attractive. I fancied him. But I'm not in love with him, for heaven's sake! It's been weeks since I've even seen him!'

Cathy's temper was fraying rapidly. So was Lorna's, but she had more control—which was just as well, because her temper was far, far worse than Cathy's. And Lorna wasn't sure whom she was angry with, her sister or this Karel person.

'Look,' Cathy was pacing around the room in agitation now, 'I'll need some money——'

'Some money?'

'For the abortion, stupid! I'll have it done privately. Nobody will know a thing about it. You know I always spend my money as I go along, so I'll sell this.' She snatched up the fox fur coat. 'This is worth a few hundred. It's brand new.'

Sadly, Lorna shook her head. Cathy had always longed for a fur coat. 'You've worked hard to buy that.'

'*I* didn't buy the coat!' Her sister's voice was scathing. 'It was a gift from an admirer.'

'Karel?'

'No. It's from a new admirer.' She looked pleased with herself now. 'As a matter of fact, it's someone involved in television. I've landed myself a smashing assignment. I'm going to be in a series of commercials for a new range of make-up. So you'll be seeing me on the box, soon! I'm moving up in the world, Lorna, and I'm not going to ruin my career for a baby I don't want.'

'It wouldn't mean——'

'That's my last word on the matter!' Cathy shrieked. 'Please go now. You're making me late!'

Lorna got to her feet. She felt desperately upset, bewildered by Cathy and the way she had changed during the past year. Dear lord, what was happening to her?

Suddenly Cathy dashed over and hugged her. 'I'm sorry—I didn't want to fight with you, Lorna. I know you mean well.'

'You are my only concern in all this.' Lorna was choked. 'You've got time. Use it to think. If you do decide to have the baby, you know you always have a home with me. After all, that was the original plan, wasn't it? That we would run the shop together?'

Cathy said nothing.

'Just ... take care. Promise me you'll think carefully?'

Finally, Cathy nodded and Lorna left without saying another word. They kissed briefly as they parted, and in their eyes there was sadness and a silent apology because they'd fought.

Lorna walked wearily down the street and got in her car, making no attempt to start it. Her mind was spinning as she sat, staring straight ahead of her without seeing anything. The row, all that Cathy had told her, was making her feel quite dizzy. Suddenly, something snapped inside her and she was filled with the kind of anger, rage, she had not felt for a long, long time. This wasn't Cathy's fault! It *wasn't* her fault!

Memories, visions of the past, raced before Lorna's eyes. Memories of their mother in the midst of a screaming row with one or other of the men she had lived with. Visions of Cathy and herself huddled in a corner, watching as their mother was struck viciously across the face. Cathy's childish, strangled sobs . . . two little girls dressed always in second-hand clothes . . . cheap housing where the damp caused the paper to peel from the walls. The constant shortage of money. The tempers which were always flaring and the rotten, no-good men, the *scroungers* who had been in their mother's life, constantly breaking their promises, constantly betting away their money, getting drunk, causing havoc.

Yet it was always the females who had suffered, never the men. And it had seemed never to end. And now . . . why should Cathy have all this upset while the man responsible sailed along obliviously? Why should he get off scot free when this was his problem as much as it was Cathy's? He'd had his fun, and according to Cathy he wouldn't be in the least interested in the result of it!

'We'll see about that!' Lorna said aloud. Men! Was there no end to their selfishness? She had driven down the street before she even realised she had done so. She paused at the junction and then she saw what she was looking for, just a hundred yards ahead of her. Knightsbridge, Cathy had said. She drove to the telephone kiosk and swung open the heavy door, reaching for the directories. Not for an instant did she stop to think what she was doing, to consider her actions. Beside herself with anger, she was quite literally seeing red, and she blinked hard in an effort to clear her vision, then found the address, the telephone number she was looking for.

The phone was answered quickly and Lorna shoved a coin into the slot at the sound of the pips. She didn't speak, she just listened. 'Van der Buren,' the voice said.

Then again, 'Van der Buren ... Hello?' So he was home!

Lorna slammed down the phone and got back into her car. The address in Knightsbridge was easy enough to find and by the time she had found a parking spot and walked to Van der Buren's home, the turmoil and haze in her mind had cleared somewhat but her anger was still very much with her.

It was a large house, tall, old and in very good repair. Lorna dashed up the four stone steps, pressed the bell and waited, shifting on her feet, agitated beyond reason.

A middle-aged woman in a somewhat old-fashioned pinafore answered the door. The cleaner, a daily woman perhaps?

'I'd like to see Mr Van der Buren,' Lorna said with a calmness that surprised her.

'Yes.' The woman nodded. 'But he isn't at home, miss.'

It would have been easy to shout at the woman, but Lorna's anger was not directed at her. And it was obvious that the cleaner had had instructions about unknown females calling at the house of the man who was becoming a well-known fashion photographer. So Lorna used her brains and she smiled very pleasantly. 'It's all right,' she assured, 'he is expecting me, actually. I've just spoken to him on the telephone.'

'Oh!' The woman's face broke into a smile. 'I'm sorry, I didn't realise you——'

'May I come in, please?' Lorna was already on the move, and the woman stepped back and held the door open for her.

She was shown into a large living room and invited to sit down, being told that Mr Van der Buren was upstairs. 'I'll tell him you're here, miss,' the woman said politely.

The cleaner left Lorna in the living room and went upstairs to Mr Van der Buren's bedroom. She knocked on the door and stepped inside when he answered.

CHAPTER TWO

Anton Van der Buren had just started packing his suitcase. He had heard the doorbell and he looked questioningly at the cleaner as she came into his room. 'What is it, Mrs Gray?'

'It's someone for you, Mr Anton. A young lady.'

'Indeed?' he smiled. 'And the young lady's name?'

'Oh! I—I didn't ask. But it isn't someone I've seen before,' she added helpfully. 'She's a tall girl, pretty, and she's got red hair.'

Anton's smile broadened. 'I think you've got your wires crossed, Mrs Gray. It sounds like someone who's looking for my cousin. A model, or a would-be model, perhaps?'

'No.' Mrs Gray shook her head firmly. 'It isn't Mr Karel she wants. I thought so at first, but no. It's the lady you've just spoken to on the telephone. I didn't think to ask her name because she says you're expecting her.'

Anton's brows rose slightly. How curious! He wasn't expecting anyone, he'd spoken to no one, but someone had tried to ring him from a public box and had been unable to get through. He was mildly intrigued.

'Very well, Mrs Gray, I'll go down.' He glanced at his watch. There was plenty of time before his flight to Amsterdam, but he had a visit to make before heading for Heathrow, and he must leave plenty of leeway to allow for the rush-hour traffic. He grunted. 'Mrs Gray, would you be kind enough to pack this case for me? Put in everything you see on the bed, except those papers, of course.'

He headed for the door, then came back again, taking a note from his wallet. 'You'll be leaving shortly, my dear. Here, have a drink on me, won't you? And many thanks.'

'Oh, Mr Anton, I shouldn't——'

'Don't be silly. Karel's house is not the easiest place to keep clean. I'm well aware of that,' he grinned.

Mrs Gray beamed at him. 'Thank you. And a safe journey home, Mr Anton. When will you be visiting again?'

'England? Or my cousin?'

'Here,' she smiled. 'I meant when will you be coming here, to the house?'

This time his smile was decidedly roguish. 'The next time Karel's away!'

Mrs Gray laughed as he left the room. Such a nice man! She glanced at the note he'd given her. A drink, he'd said. He'd given her enough for a bottle! And that was just what she would buy with it, too. Mr Anton had never stayed here this long before, not for two weeks on the trot. But then he wouldn't have this time either if Mr Karel hadn't been in Africa for the past ten days. Funny, she thought, how very different the two men were—chalk and cheese! Not that it was any of her business, of course.

Lorna had not bothered to sit down, she was too eager to confront Karel Van der Buren to make herself comfortable. Comfortable? In this room? The place was horrible, horrible! Oh, it had no doubt cost a lot of money to decorate and furnish. Or should she say to *get up*? It would be better described as a get-up. It was a big room and it was full of gimmicks, spotlights zoomed on to dozens of framed photographs—nudes mostly—and it had a sort of divan thing built into the curve of the window, stacked with plump, multi-coloured cushions. The old fireplace made a mockery of all the ultra-modern paraphernalia and spoke of a grace and elegance this house must once have been endowed with. But that was gone now, lamentably.

So this was Karel Van der Buren's bachelor pad? Lorna thrust her hands into the pockets of her coat and shot a distasteful look at the divan. How very convenient! No need to walk upstairs. Oh, it was a fine room in which to practise a seduction routine—if the girl concerned happened to like this sort of atmosphere. She spun round as she heard the door open.

Anton paused in his tracks, no longer mildly intrigued but very much so. Mrs Gray had been way off beam in her brief description of his visitor. Yes, the girl was tall, but not remarkably so. Her hair, however, was not red but the colour of copper, burnished copper. As she moved slightly, he had to amend that and found himself reminded of the rustic colours of autumn—the highlights in her hair were myriad. Natural, too, as the soft, short waves appeared to be.

She was not pretty, either. She was, he thought, very beautiful. She was also very angry. True, he didn't know her from Adam, but those eyes! They were large, not needing the make-up she'd put on them, delicate though it was. Those eyes would speak for themselves, and right now they were sparkling with unmistakable anger.

Anton closed the door softly behind him. 'I understand you wish to talk to me?'

Lorna stiffened. The sight of him came as a shock to her. Quite what she'd imagined ... well, she hadn't paused to do that. But she had certainly expected someone younger. Good grief, this man was years older than Cathy! He must have been in his mid, perhaps late thirties, and not to her knowledge did Cathy have a predilection for older men.

More shocking was the way he was dressed. In a dark, conventional suit with a crisp white shirt and a tie, one would envisage him spending his days in a smart city office rather than in a darkroom or clicking his camera at fashion models.

As for his living room ... not only had its spaciousness suddenly diminished but it ... it just didn't go with its owner. It didn't fit. Or he didn't fit. In no way did he look like what he was, and if this room was a reflection of his personality, Lorna could only conclude that there were two distinct sides to it. Everyone had heard of Dr Jekyll and Mr Hyde.

'You are Mr Van der Buren?'

'I am.' He walked towards her, his hand extended. 'I don't believe we've met before. And you are ...?' He smiled at her, knowing they had never met before. He would not have forgotten!

Lorna's sense of shock was renewed. Something inside her recoiled; she wanted to step back, away from him. But that was a feeling she was very familiar with. His size didn't help. He towered over her by some six inches in spite of the high-heeled court shoes she was wearing.

Most disturbing of all was his smile, because as he smiled she was forced to acknowledge his attractiveness. It had been undeniable at first glance, but when he smiled, it changed his entire countenance and revealed beautifully white, even teeth.

Lorna did not step back. She didn't move at all. She kept her hands where they were, in her pockets, ignored the hand he was proffering and looked him straight in the eyes. 'I'm Cathy's sister.'

'Cathy? I'm sorry, I don't know a Cathy——'

The words had barely left his mouth before she answered that one. 'Oh, really?' Her voice was like ice. 'Then let me refresh your memory! The name is Brenner. Cathy Brenner—the tall, blonde girl who is now expecting your baby!'

'*What?* I'm afraid you're making a mistake. I'm not responsible for——'

Lorna pulled her hands free and flung her arms about wildly. 'The model you seduced some time ago in this plastic parlour of yours! The girl you plied with alcohol!'

She saw recognition dawn on his face, but his next words drove her crazy. 'You're making a mistake. Miss Brenner, you're talking to the wrong man. I'm not——'

Incensed, Lorna gave him no chance to finish, to *lie*. She didn't give him time to draw breath. 'You bastard!

Are you so much in demand that you can't remember who you have and have not slept with? My sister isn't mistaken about when she got pregnant, if *that's* what you're about to imply! So don't try to place the responsibility elsewhere! Cathy is nineteen years old, Van der Buren, and you——'

The shrill ringing of a trimphone on a nearby table stopped her in mid-sentence. She turned, glaring at it, and then at the man who was standing just a few yards from her. Why the hell didn't he *say* something, or answer the phone, at least! Why was he just standing there, staring at her as if she were some sort of specimen?

Anton said nothing. Damn Karel! What sort of mess had he got himself into? And it was not the first time, either. Something similar had happened to his young cousin when he was seventeen. The idiot!

It was the girl Anton felt sorry for. Not necessarily Cathy Brenner so much as *this* girl, this beautiful, protective sister of hers. Never had he seen someone so angry, so incredibly upset. He picked up the phone, his mind racing, thinking about all this as he spoke.

Lorna turned away in disgust. But at least the man had had the good grace to look concerned. Not that it lessened her fury—and the frustration of being interrupted wasn't helping her. She wanted to get this over with and get out of the place. This room was setting her teeth on edge.

God, he was cool! He was rabbiting away in a language she didn't understand now. Dutch, probably. His name was Dutch, wasn't it? She turned to look at him, hitching her bag on to her shoulder and looking pointedly at her watch.

Attractive, the man certainly was. Which was just the word her sister had used, not handsome. In the conventional sense, he would not be described as handsome. In his hair there was more than a smattering of grey, though it was mainly dark blond and was thick. His eyes deceived because they were a warm shade of brown and they gave the impression of honesty, of openness. If Lorna had met him in different circumstances, she would have judged him to be something quite different from what she knew him to be.

She could understand Cathy being attracted by him, regardless of his age. Physically, he had it all, a broad, solid body, the sort of height which would make even Cathy feel petite, rugged, attractive features which would make any woman look twice. And didn't he know it! How he exploited his assets! What had Cathy called him? A womaniser, among other things. Well, that much fitted, at least.

As he put the phone down, Lorna continued as if the interruption had never taken place. 'Cathy is nineteen years old, Van der Buren, and you are old enough to be her father! How do you *feel* about that? How do you feel when I tell you she's thinking of having an abortion? You have remembered who she is now? You'd better!' she finished viciously.

For a long moment, he just looked at her. 'Distressed,' he said at length, his voice very quiet. 'I'm distressed by all of this.' But the girl was more distressed. She looked fit to kill, or was that shine in her eyes an indication that she was about to burst into tears? Whatever, her last outburst had reinforced the decision he had made minutes ago. He would not tell her of the mistake she was making as far as he was concerned.

He deemed it wiser not to do that, for several reasons. Karel was his cousin, when all was said and done, and he would rather Karel heard about all this from himself than from an hysterical woman. Secondly, the girl had finished her tirade with something which sounded like a threat, and he did not quite know how to interpret that. So the best thing was to try to placate her. For her own sake, too, he wanted to placate her. And after all the personal abuse she'd flung at him, if he told her now he was not the man she thought he was, she would feel a complete idiot. He had tried to disabuse her earlier, but she wouldn't give him a chance to speak. And now the situation had run away with them both.

With that part of his mind that stood detached from all this, Anton was wishing he had met this girl in different circumstances. He wondered what she was really like, when she was behaving normally. Beyond the anger there was something about her that intrigued him, and that had nothing to do with her physical beauty.

'Miss Brenner, please, can we talk about this calmly? Won't you sit down?'

He was gesturing towards the divan. 'I'll stand.' He kept calling her 'Miss Brenner', but she didn't bother to tell him her name was Stewart. That she and Cathy had had different fathers was hardly relevant to this matter. 'I'd like to know what you propose to do. I've told you Cathy's intentions.'

'Is she likely to change her mind?'

'That's for *you* to find out!'

'What ... do you expect me to do?' Anton was careful to keep the right tone, to ask the question gently. He had no wish to upset the girl further. Nonetheless, she misunderstood him and went up in the air.

'You can get round there and talk to her! Cathy's not in love with you any more than you're in love with her, so I doubt that she'll expect you to do the honourable thing. Frankly, I'm glad about that, because I wouldn't fancy you as a brother-in-law! But this is your problem just as much as it's hers—so go and sort it out!'

'Understood.' He nodded, realising he had no chance whatever of placating her. 'Tell me, why didn't Cathy come here herself?'

'She said you wouldn't be in the least interested. Charming, that, isn't it? I'm glad to see she'd exaggerated somewhat. Anyway, *I've* told you. Now the ball's in your court. Don't bother to see me to the door, and I can't say I'm pleased to have met you. You know

where to find my sister, and if you can't remember her
phone number then I suggest you look in your little
black book! Goodbye.'

Lorna flounced out of the room, slamming the door
so hard that it rattled on its hinges. A moment later,
Anton grinned as he heard her give the outer door a
similar treatment. What an exquisitely *female* female!
And what a temper!

But his grin quickly faded and he lowered himself
into a wicker chair, hearing it creak under his weight.
What day was this, for heaven's sake? Thursday. Thank
goodness Karel was due home tomorrow! He had spent
the past ten days in Africa, taking photographs against
exotic backgrounds. But there was no way Anton could
reach him immediately. He looked at his watch. Karel
would have boarded his homeward flight by now.
Damn!

He got up quickly and headed for the room which
Karel used as a study. Twenty minutes later he left a
sealed envelope propped against the electric kettle in the
kitchen, with Karel's name and the word 'personal'
written boldly on the front of it. He could have written
reams about the encounter he'd just had with Cathy
Brenner's sister, but time would not permit. So he had
kept strictly to the facts and had made no personal
comment whatever.

Karel would do all he could to help Cathy Brenner,
Anton was confident of that. He might be a rather zany
young man, but he had a soft heart, most especially
where beautiful women were concerned.

What was the sister's first name? If only he'd been able
to ask her! If only Mrs Gray had thought to ask! Still, he
had her surname, that was the main thing. He could look
her up in the telephone directory. He would ring every
Brenner listed until he reached her. But not yet!

Anton had every intention of seeing her again, but
not yet. He would have to give her plenty of time to
cool off. He would have to wait until this business
between Cathy and Karel had been resolved—however

they chose to do it. And strictly speaking it was their business and no one else's.

On his next visit to England he would phone Cathy's sister and invite her to dinner. There was no reason why she shouldn't be receptive by then, since things would have sorted themselves out—mistaken identity and all!

Lorna tried umpteen times to ring Cathy during Friday and Saturday, but there was no reply. She wanted to know what Karel Van der Buren had said. At a little after ten on Sunday morning she tried again, and still there was no answer. Where the devil was Cathy? She wouldn't be working on a Sunday.

She discovered her sister's whereabouts soon enough when the doorbell rang about half an hour later and she found Cathy, white-faced, standing on her doorstep. 'Cathy! What on earth . . .' Lorna's voice trailed off as she realised her sister was fit to drop. Without make-up her face was always pale, but right now it was as white as a sheet.

'Cathy, Cathy—what have you done?' She took hold of her arm and led her to the stairs at the back of the shop.

'Nothing! Nothing, honestly!' Cathy shook her head and held tightly on to the banister as she started to climb. She sank wearily into an armchair in Lorna's living room, her hands trembling on her lap. 'I've had a miscarriage, Lorna, and I—I . . .' She started weeping, quietly, almost noiselessly.

Lorna made some tea and set the tray down on the rug by the fire. She sat quietly until her sister was ready to talk.

'Ironic, isn't it?' Cathy's voice was hardly more than a whisper. 'The matter has been taken out of my hands.'

'When did this happen?'

'Just after midnight last night—this morning.'

'Good grief! Cathy, why didn't you . . . how did you get here?'

'By taxi.' Cathy shrugged. 'It cost me a fortune.'

Lorna shook her head, incredulous. Was there no end to her sister's irresponsibility, her self-neglect? 'You should have phoned me. You shouldn't have made the journey here! You idiot! You've got to see a doctor, Cathy. If you'd phoned me, I'd have come to you, you know that. I just don't understand you these days. Honestly! What are you trying——' She stopped short at the look on Cathy's face, forcing herself to shut up. In Lorna's opinion the girl was due for a good telling off—but not now. She looked utterly, utterly weary.

'I didn't want to stay in my flat. I don't want anyone to see me like this. And I don't want a doctor—I'll be okay.'

'Come on,' Lorna sighed, 'I'm putting you to bed. You need a damn good rest. That's a word you don't know the meaning of, isn't it?' She bit her lip as she helped Cathy to her feet. There she was again, nagging!

There was a single spare bed in Lorna's room, but it wasn't made up. She put Cathy into her own bed and went immediately to phone the doctor, not bothering to argue about it. Lorna's doctor was a kindly man in middle age. He would see Cathy as an emergency patient.

Actually, Cathy made no protest when Lorna announced Dr Smith's arrival. She left them alone and went to peel some vegetables for lunch. It seemed like an age before the doctor emerged from the bedroom. Lorna glanced at her watch when he eventually came to speak to her. He *had* been an age.

'I've read your sister the riot act,' he began.

Lorna motioned him to sit down. 'Good. I'd planned on doing that myself.'

The doctor's smile was brief. 'She tells me she's a model.'

'That's right. And it's hard work, contrary to what you might imagine. She loves it, of course, but she goes out every night of the week, she hasn't had a holiday, she smokes a lot, she drinks a lot and she eats very little.'

Dr Smith's cheeks puffed out as he blew out a long breath. 'The latter is very obvious. Frankly, I'm not surprised she miscarried. I wouldn't go so far as to say she's undernourished, but——'

'But what?' Lorna looked at him anxiously. 'She hasn't got anorexia?'

'No. But if she doesn't start eating properly, regularly, she's heading for trouble. I've told her this, Miss Stewart. I've also told her that with a balanced diet she can give her body all the nutriment it needs without putting on weight. I do think she's anaemic, however, and she's promised to see her own doctor for some tests and a thorough examination. In the meantime . . .'

'In the meantime, I'm keeping her with me for a while,' Lorna put in.

'Good.' He got to his feet. 'I've left a prescription with her. Get it for her tomorrow, would you? And see that she stays in bed for a few days. Your sister is very run down, Miss Stewart.'

Cathy was subdued to the point of depression for the next couple of days and Lorna refrained from questioning her or nagging at her. She was willing to eat, though, which pleased Lorna no end. Only when Cathy got up for a few hours one evening during the week did she tell Lorna what had been going through her mind. She vowed she would turn over a new leaf, that from now on she would eat properly, see that she had enough sleep and take everything else in moderation.

'That doctor frightened me, Lorna, I can tell you. Apart from all that, I—I don't want to find myself . . . you know. I don't want anything like this to happen to me again. But I was very unlucky.'

'I don't see what luck has to do with it.' Lorna handed her a hot drink and turned the gas fire as high as it would go. November was fast approaching and the weather had turned really cold.

'I was unlucky!' Cathy protested. 'It was the first time

I'd forgotten to take my pill and look what happened! If that's not rotten luck, I don't know what is!'

'You forgot your pill because you were drunk, remember?'

Cathy fell silent. There was no answer to that, and Lorna was always disapproving these days.

'Now, tell me what happened with Karel.'

'Karel!' Cathy laughed for the first time in days. 'Karel was furious with you. Absolutely furious!'

Lorna had an instant mental picture of the man. She couldn't imagine him being furious. He had seemed like such a cool customer. 'The feeling's mutual, I'm sure.'

'That isn't fair.' Cathy's face had a stubborn look about it now. 'If you want me to talk about this, please keep quiet and stop being so stuffy and disapproving. Please bear in mind that I'm nineteen and no longer your responsibility.' More gently, she added, 'You've done more than enough for me in the past. You know I'm grateful to you for all that, but you've got to face the fact that we're different, you and I. We think differently. I don't harp on at you and your single-mindedness about money, or over your hatred of men. I understand you. I understand why you are the way you are.

'I want the same understanding from you. I've told you I'm going to straighten myself out, and I will. I'm not the idiot you take me for. I've still got my dreams, all the dreams I used to tell you about when I was a kid. You had your dreams, too, and you've got what you wanted—your lovely shop. You got it in your own way, but I never nagged you for working all the hours God sent.

'You're interfering in my life too much, Lorna. I've told you this before. You don't approve if I happen to take a few short cuts in getting what I want. You should have seen the look on your face when I told you a man had bought me that fox fur coat! What of it, anyway? Just because you won't accept the time of day from a man, it doesn't mean I have to be the same.

David can give me as many presents as he likes, and I won't complain! He can well afford to. Quite apart from his fabulous job, he's independently rich. He's taking me on holiday at Christmas, by the way. He's got a villa in the Canary Islands and we're having three weeks in the sun! Then we're starting work on those television commercials I told you about.

'Now, let's get this clear: I'm not going to make myself ill, I'm not going to get pregnant again, but I *am* going to enjoy myself. And I don't want to argue with you about my lifestyle. I hate fighting with you, Lorna, you're all I have in the world and I want us to be friends. So please accept me as I am.'

It was quite a speech. Lorna sipped thoughtfully at her drink, wondering how to answer it. Please accept me as I am, Cathy had said. There was no choice in the matter. Cathy had been foolish lately, she'd made a few mistakes, but at least she'd realised them. Basically, though, she wouldn't change. Lorna knew this. Before she had a chance to speak, however, Cathy went on.

Her voice was calm and reasonable, but she continued to stress the point about Lorna's interference. 'You shouldn't have gone to Karel's house. It wasn't your place to do that. This is what I mean about your interference. What you did was going too far.'

'I—yes.' Lorna could not deny it. It had been Cathy's place to tell Van der Buren, not hers. She had thought about this several times. But it was too late, and her only excuse was the rage she'd been in. 'I was so angry, Cathy, I didn't stop to think. And I couldn't bear the idea of Karel getting off scot free, going merrily on his way while you——'

'Don't be daft! I'd have told him, sure enough!'

'But you said——'

'I wasn't thinking straight on Thursday. I'm no martyr. I'm not the type to suffer in silence!'

'But you were so——'

'I told you,' Cathy waved a slender hand in the air. 'I wasn't thinking straight. Besides, Karel could easily have afforded to help me—whatever I decided to do. And he offered to do just that, Lorna, so don't think too harshly of him. He came to see me on Saturday night and we talked things over civilly. He was willing to do anything he could to help me, but I—we—were realistic. We are not in love with each other, neither of us is ready for marriage, so marriage didn't enter the question. He took me out to dinner and it was all very nice. I'd only been home an hour or so when—when I took ill.'

Lorna made a conscious effort to keep any harshness from her voice. 'Don't bite my head off, Cathy, but what was wrong with Thursday night, or Friday? Why didn't Karel come to see you then? Why did he wait till Saturday night?'

'Because he was still in Africa. He should have got home on Friday, but there was some sort of hitch and he had to work another day. Besides, I was out with David on Thursday and Friday.'

Lorna didn't hear the last sentence. '*Africa?* Africa! He wasn't in Africa! What sort of story has he given you? He was in Knightsbridge on Thursday afternoon!'

The conversation had gone back to square one and Cathy started laughing again. 'It wasn't a story. How typically cynical of you!' She picked up the hot drink Cathy had given her. 'What's this?'

'Cathy, what the devil are you talking about? I spoke to Karel face to face on Thursday, I tell you. . . . Stop pulling that face, and drink up. It's cocoa, it'll do you good.'

'Yuk!' Dutifully Cathy drank up. She was deliberately teasing Lorna, and Lorna knew it.

'Are you going to keep me waiting all night?'

Cathy grinned. 'The man you spoke to was not Karel.'

Almost leaping from her chair, Lorna stared at her. 'Of course it was Karel! I specifically asked if he were Van der Buren before I said a word!'

At that, Cathy cracked up with laughter. 'He was—

is—Van der Buren. It was Karel's cousin Anton, you idiot! And Karel was hopping mad because you told him everything!' She paused for breath, giving full vent to her laughter. 'But I made him see the funny side of it!'

'I'm glad you think it's funny,' Lorna said stiffly.

Cathy sobered somewhat. 'Sorry. But what I don't understand is, why didn't this cousin put you right? Why didn't he tell you you were talking to the wrong man?'

Thursday's scene was playing back through Lorna's mind like a film. Unconsciously, she put her hands to her face, her cheeks growing warmer by the second. 'He tried to,' she said at length. 'Come to think of it, he tried to. But I—I wasn't myself. I didn't let him get a word in.'

'I can imagine,' her sister quipped. Then, seeing Lorna's blush, which was so totally out of character, she attempted to soothe her. 'Hey, Lorna, don't worry about it! I can well imagine the choice things you said to him, but Anton lives in Amsterdam, according to Karel. So you're never going to bump into him again.'

'Thank heaven for that!' Lorna got to her feet, shaking her head wearily.

Cathy looked up in surprise. That was hardly the retort she had expected from Lorna. She had expected her to say she wouldn't give a damn if the man lived right next door to her.

'I'm going to bed, Cathy. I'm shattered. Are you coming?'

'I'll be along in a few minutes. I'm just going to ring David—I said I'd ring again tonight.'

'Where does he think you are—this David?'

Cathy tossed her hair back from her face, grinning mischievously. 'Oh, he knows I'm staying with you, and I've told the manageress of my agency the same story. I've told them you've got 'flu and I'm looking after you and your shop for a week. I hope you don't mind?'

And what difference, Lorna wondered, would it make

if she did mind? Cathy would never change. Never. Any more than Lorna would. She had been right earlier on -they should just accept each other for what they were. It would make life much simpler.

Lorna got into bed feeling unusually tired. She was also confused and bewildered over the behaviour of the man called Anton. It didn't last long, though. Within minutes she had drifted off. It just wasn't in her nature to lose sleep thinking about a man.

CHAPTER THREE

'IT isn't exactly what I had in mind . . . but it's not bad!' Eve Summers surveyed herself in the full-length mirror in the changing room at *Feline*.

Lorna suppressed a smile. The dress suited Eve perfectly, couldn't she see that? She had asked Lorna to find her something spectacular for the engagement party, and Lorna had found just that. 'It's a classic style, Eve. You can't go wrong with that sort of thing. Or is it not spectacular enough?'

Eve grinned at her. 'It is, it is. It's the colour I'm worrying about, not the style. Did you buy this especially with me in mind?'

'Of course. But don't let that influence you. I'll sell it easily enough—Christmas is coming!'

Christmas was, in fact, over three weeks away, but Eve wanted to get her dress in good time and she was not the easiest person to please.

Eve was frowning now, pulling her face as if she were making the decision of a lifetime. 'It's very—red!'

'For your colouring it's perfect, Eve. I wish I could wear that shade. But I can't. It would scream at my hair!'

At that, Eve held her own hair up and her frown cleared somewhat. 'Mm. It'd look better with my hair up, don't you think?'

Lorna cocked an eyebrow at her, grinning. 'I'd taken that much for granted. You couldn't just leave your hair dangling when you've got a neckline like that to show off.'

'Dangling?' Eve looked nonplussed. 'Is that what my hair does?'

'Frankly, yes. That style doesn't suit you one bit.'

'Lorna, you are awful! I wear it like this because it

41

makes me look younger. I'm going to be thirty this month, but I don't want to look thirty!'

'You don't look thirty.' Lorna was being honest. 'And I won't influence you in the slightest, we both know that. But do me a favour—take a look at the dress in daylight. These artificial lights don't do it justice. Come out into the shop.'

Suddenly inspired, Eve held up her hand. 'I've got a better idea. I'll let Julian decide. I do like the dress, Lorna, but——'

'But you want to please Julian.'

'Well . . .' Eve looked slightly embarrassed at that. 'You think I'm making a terrible fuss, don't you?'

'Not at all.' Lorna meant it, too. Eve was excited, and why not? It wasn't every day a girl celebrated her birthday and got engaged at the same time. Eve deserved her happiness, was entitled to a little fuss. She was a very nice person.

Lorna was quite content to let Eve take the dress back to the solicitors' offices so she might show it to her fiancé. No sooner had she gone than Mrs Miller came in with the alterations. Mrs Miller was an expert seamstress and Lorna was very, very lucky to have found such a person locally. She wouldn't trust many people to alter clothes so perfectly.

Business was good. The party season had already started and Dulcie was working four days a week until Christmas was over. Right now Dulcie was dealing with someone who was being particularly difficult, but Lorna did not interfere. Dulcie would cope.

Life was normal again, except that it was busier. Frankly, Lorna had been glad when her sister had gone back to London at the end of that dreadful week. She had peace again.

She was serving a teenager with a fancy belt which was obviously going to be someone's Christmas present, when Eve reappeared. She winked at Lorna and waited till she had finished serving.

'Julian says you're a woman of good taste and discernment.'

Lorna's face broke into a smile. 'He approved?'

'He says you have far better dress sense than I have,' Eve said in an attitude of mock jealousy.

'And what,' Lorna asked, 'did you say to that?'

'I asked him why he didn't marry you instead.'

'Eve!'

'I didn't, I didn't!' The older girl laughed heartily. 'I might not have liked his answer! Still, it will happen to you, you know.'

'Now what are you talking about?'

'This ... this euphoria. This love business. Oh, I know all about being devoted to one's career, but you'll see. The mighty will fall! I mean, look at you. You're too attractive for your own good. How long do you think you'll get away with it?'

'Get away with it?'

'Don't act daft. You know what I mean—being single!'

For the rest of my life, Lorna said silently. To Eve, she said, 'I'm going to have my euphoria right now when I take your cheque.'

'You're hard, Lorna! Hard through and through. And avaricious with it!'

'That's true. You'd better sit down.' Lorna took Eve's arm and led her to the chair near the cash desk.

Eve threw back her head and roared with laughter. 'You are dreadful, Lorna! Anyhow, you don't scare me. The price tag was on the dress and I've left Julian staring at it. He's paying!'

'Good for you!'

'So,' Eve said impishly, her eyes roving around the shop, 'I've got plenty of money to spend on something new for Christmas and New Year.'

She pulled a dress off one of the garment rails, and Lorna shook her head firmly. 'Put that back, Eve. I wouldn't sell it to you. Firstly the material doesn't warrant the price and secondly it's just not you.'

Eve promptly put it back. 'Have you got yourself anything new for Christmas? Are you and your sister going anywhere nice?'

'Cathy is,' Lorna answered without thinking. 'She's spending Christmas abroad. She's having three weeks in the sun.' It wasn't that she minded telling Eve this titbit, it was just that she had forgotten about Eve's invitation to spend Christmas with her—or rather, with her and her parents.

Eve extended the invitation again, having learned that Cathy would be away and Lorna would be on her own. They discussed the matter for five minutes or more, but Lorna was very reluctant to accept.

'I'm grateful, Eve, really. It's very kind of you but, believe it or not, I'd feel very shy about going to stay with people I don't know.'

Eve looked at Dulcie, who couldn't help overhearing all this. Dulcie looked at Eve. Then the pair of them looked at Lorna and said, '*Shy?*'

'You, shy?'

'Since when?'

Between them, they overrode Lorna's protests. Eve assured her that she would be one of several houseguests, that her parents loved having company, and Dulcie—well, Dulcie was horrified at the idea of Lorna spending Christmas on her own.

When Eve had gone, Dulcie offered to open the shop on New Year's Eve in order that Lorna might stay at the Summers' home until New Year's Day. If last year was anything to go by, New Year's Eve should be quite profitable. There were always the ladies who wanted that last-minute new dress for some dinner-do or other.

'There's no point in you driving back from Hampshire,' Dulcie pointed out, 'when I'm here in Windsor. I'll cope perfectly well, don't worry.'

'Well, aren't you going out yourself?' Lorna asked, grateful for the older woman's loyalty and interest.

'Yes, but I'll have bags of time to get ready. I only live five minutes' drive away, don't forget.'

Once the decision was made, Lorna found herself quite looking forward to it, strangely enough. She hadn't relished the idea of spending Christmas Day alone. Christmas was such a . . . well, of all the days of the year, Christmas was a day when one shouldn't be alone. Even Lorna felt that, self-sufficient as she was.

'You'll have a lovely week at the Summers' house,' Dulcie finished, pleased that Lorna was going. 'I believe they're very nice people. Eve's father is the architect, you know, and he——' She broke off as the doorbell tinkled and shot a quick look at Lorna. 'It's that awkward so-and-so I spent over an hour with earlier,' she whispered. 'She's brought that suit back! What do you bet?'

'I'll deal with her,' Lorna smiled. 'You get yourself some lunch, Dulcie. Bring me a roast beef sandwich, will you? With mustard.'

On Saturday night Lorna brought her books up to date. She was no mathematician, but she knew how many beans make five. Her education had been minimal; in the type of schools Lorna had gone to the teachers had needed to spend most of their time striving for some sort of discipline. And for one reason or another she had been shifted from pillar to post as a child, never attending the same school for any length of time.

But education and intelligence are not the same thing, and Lorna had plenty of intelligence. She learned something new every day and she read all sorts of books in her spare time. In the university of life she had learned plenty, and when it came to weighing people up she was usually accurate.

She rarely made a mistake when it came to filling in her VAT returns, checking the discount she was entitled to for prompt payment to her suppliers, or giving change in the shop. She had been cheated in business once, when she was younger and vulnerable because of her ignorance, and that had taught her to be very cautious.

She switched off her calculator and got up from her desk, thinking about the man who had cheated her. At the time, it had seemed like a vast sum of money he had taken, but by today's standards it wasn't, of course. Still, that was hardly the point. It had been Lorna's money and she had needed it desperately.

In the kitchen there was a bottle of brandy, good brandy, and she decided to have a glass by way of celebration. *Feline* had been open for exactly one year and it was doing well. She had realised her dream. Next year she would make a substantial profit. This year her profits were minimal because there had been so much to pay out for—the smart, tasteful fascia on the shop front, the garment rails, fixtures and fittings, the counter, the cash till. Still, apart from her outstanding invoices for recent purchases, the stock was paid for. And she had bought a good quality, fitted carpet for her living room, bedroom and bathroom.

She looked down at the rose-coloured carpet, at the chintz three-piece suite. Soon she would buy the lamps and coffee tables she wanted, she would have the bathroom re-tiled and get herself a new bed. All in good time. For now, things were taking shape very nicely. Next year she would be able to afford a holiday—just about. She had never been abroad, she had never had a proper holiday in her life. Perhaps she would take a week off.

Cathy's remark came floating back to her, about her singlemindedness over money. Lorna didn't want money for money's sake. She wanted, needed, what money represented. It gave one independence, freedom, and that was what she wanted. She needed the feeling of security it gave, most especially. She was perfectly happy to spend it as long as she was making more and as long as she had a reserve to fall back on—just in case. She never wanted to have to rely on someone else for her living and she never again wanted to go short of something she needed. Cathy understood all this, really.

Sitting by the fire, sipping her brandy, Lorna

suddenly found herself crying. Quite unaccountably, she realised there were tears on her cheeks. In one swallow she finished her drink and refilled the glass, switching on the radio on her way to the kitchen, impatient with herself. What the devil was the matter with her? Why the tears, when she had just celebrated having achieved what she had worked so hard to achieve—her dream? Tears of happiness they might have been, but Lorna despised herself for them. She simply was not the tearful type. Good grief, she hadn't shown such softness since ... since her unforgettable experience with Jake Dougan.

It wasn't all that far to the home of Eve's parents, the problem was that Lorna couldn't find the place. She had turned off the main road past Alton, as Eve had told her to, and had been driving along country lanes getting more and more lost. She had the sneaking feeling that if she carried on like this she would end up in Winchester!

At the first telephone box she came to, Lorna got out of her car to look up the name Summers. There couldn't be many of them around here; she would ring, tell Eve where she was and ask her to come and fetch her.

There were no directories in the box!

It was ten o'clock on Christmas morning and Lorna had no idea whether Directory Enquiries would be operating today. The question became irrelevant when she picked up the telephone receiver and found that the phone was as dead as a doornail. She was just thinking there wasn't much sign of life around here at all when she spotted a youngster walking his dog.

'Excuse me!' she called out to him, running to catch him up. 'I'm looking for a house called The Lions. You wouldn't happen to know where it is, would you? It can't be far away——'

'Of course. That's Sir Michael's house.' Politely, in a very upper-class accent, the boy told her it was less than half a mile down the road.

Lorna looked at him in confusion. 'Sir Michael?'

'You did say you wanted The Lions? Sir Michael Summers' house?'

'Er—yes.' Lorna's heart sank. Eve's father was a *Sir*? She'd had no idea! Worse than that was the realisation that she had already driven past the house twice. At the foot of the drive there were two life-sized lions, mounted, carved from stone. She just hadn't put two and two together because the house at the top of the drive was so vast it never entered her head that it was the place she had been invited to for the Christmas and New Year holidays.

'I've—er—just remembered where it is. Thank you.' She wished the boy a merry Christmas, and if he thought her a little strange, he showed no sign of it.

Lorna brought her car to a halt and switched off the engine. She looked from one lion to the next at the foot of the drive, feeling quite idiotic. But that was nothing compared to the nervousness, the apprehension which had suddenly removed every last ounce of her confidence.

The drive was very long and as straight as an arrow. There was nothing to obscure the view of the house from where she was parked. She couldn't stay *here*! With a Sir and a Lady—a houseful of strangers with whom she would have nothing at all in common? She looked at the house at the top of the drive, knowing an unfair, irrational annoyance with Eve. Why hadn't she said this was her parents' *country seat*? Why hadn't she said her parents were titled?

Because Eve took it all for granted, that's why. Eve was in no way at fault. No wonder she was always spending money; she *had* money! Lorna had guessed that Eve came from a well-to-do family . . . but *this*?

Crazy thoughts tumbled through her mind. She wished her car were not so old; she wished she'd washed it before leaving Windsor. She wished she made a habit of watching the news, just in case someone asked her what she thought about some current event or other. She wished she'd flatly refused this invitation—and the one to the engagement party.

Her imagination ran riot, envisaging questions which would come politely from these hospitable strangers. 'Tell us about yourself, Lorna,' they would say, looking at her expectantly. 'We understand you run a ladies' dress shop? And what did you do with yourself before that? What part of the country do you come from, actually? Were your parents in business?'

Lorna started the engine and put the car into reverse. She moved it backwards about five yards and then stopped again. Damn it all, what on earth was she thinking about? She couldn't run away! And why should she? She was invited, she was expected. She had been out of her depth before, but she had coped. Life had never yet presented her with a situation she had not been able to surmount. Even Jake Dougan hadn't managed to do that to her.

She caught sight of herself in the driving mirror, then she looked down at the beautiful dress she was wearing. It was silk, the colour of oysters, and she knew she looked good in it—and her make-up was just right. She would grace anyone's dining table, Sir Michael and Lady Summers' included.

She thrust the gear lever into first and drove confidently up the drive.

Eve appeared on the steps of the front entrance before Lorna had brought the car to a halt. 'Hi!' She gave Lorna a hug, telling her to leave the keys in the car. 'Someone will park it for you. Just leave all your luggage and everything, one of the maids will unpack for you. And Merry Christmas! Did you find us easily enough? Were my directions okay?'

'Merry Christmas! Yes—er—well, I took one wrong turning.'

She was ushered indoors by the older girl, who was chattering ten to the dozen. 'We're eating at one. Can't wait, can you? Come into the drawing room and meet

Mummy and Daddy. It's turned incredibly cold, hasn't it? Did you have a good day yesterday?'

'Record-breaking.' Lorna laughed, feeling more at ease by the second. She was introduced to Eve's parents in the huge drawing room in which there stood a beautifully decorated Christmas tree, the biggest Lorna had seen outside Trafalgar Square.

'Am I the last to arrive?' she asked Lady Summers.

'No, dear,' she smiled. 'We're still waiting for my aunt Mary.'

'My great-aunt,' Eve put in. 'She's always the last to arrive. She's very old, so we make allowances.'

Lorna was seated by a roaring log fire and asked what she would like to drink, watching with suppressed amusement as Eve's father reached for an old-fashioned bell-pull near the fireplace. Fancy having servants to look after you!

Sir Michael was a smallish, balding man with a ruddy complexion and a friendly face. 'Where is everyone?' he asked Eve. 'Where's Julian? Is he hung over from last night or is he avoiding me for some reason?'

'Hung over, Daddy. Right first time.'

When the door of the drawing room opened, Lorna expected to see a maid or a butler, perhaps, appearing in response to Sir Michael's summons.

It was neither.

'Ah, there you are!' Sir Michael said heartily. He marched across the room and slipped an arm around the shoulder of the man who had just come in—which wasn't all that easy because Sir Michael was considerably shorter.

'Let me introduce you to our new arrival.' Eve's father beamed at the man, and Lorna didn't move a muscle. Whether it was expected that she stand up and offer her hand—whether it would be right and proper to do that—she didn't know. She knew only that she wished herself invisible.

She was face to face with Anton Van der Buren.

CHAPTER FOUR

LORNA'S shock was followed instantly by disappointment and then embarrassment. She was plunged back in
time, hearing her own voice shrieking in anger. It
drowned out the introduction Sir Michael was making.
She could see Anton Van der Buren smiling at her, the
laughter dancing in his eyes, and she simply did not
know what to do with herself. Dread rendered her
incapable of moving. What was he going to say? What
was he going to *say* in front of these people?

He moved towards her, his hand extended, and
somehow she managed to lift her own hand from the
arm of her chair. But she couldn't speak, and the last
thing she expected was for him to lift her hand to his
lips and gently kiss the back of it. 'I'm delighted . . .
enchanted . . . to meet you, Miss—Stewart.'

Telling herself she deserved this sarcasm did not help
Lorna to cope with it. She glanced round swiftly in an
effort to see how everyone else was reacting. Lady
Summers was smiling, Sir Michael was taking a
decanter from a maid who had just come in and Eve
was grinning like a Cheshire cat. 'This is Anton being
his most charming,' she put in with a giggle.

Lorna's eyes met with his as he straightened, looking
down at her. 'I—Mr Van der Buren . . . how—how do
you do?'

'Anton, please,' he said graciously. 'Such a mouthful,
isn't it, Mr Van der Buren?' The emphasis he put on his
last few words was meant solely for her, of course. As
was the emphasis he'd put on her surname.

Sir Michael, who was attending to the drinks himself,
broke the tension. 'I should amend that introduction,
Lorna. Anton is not only a very dear friend of the
family, he's also about to take over my business.'

'Don't jump the gun, Michael.' Anton seated himself next to Lady Summers. 'I haven't made a decision yet.'

'Ach!' Sir Michael waved the words away without consideration. 'You're too young to drop out, Anton. I wish you'd stop talking like that!'

'I wish you two would stop talking like *this*!' Lady Summers laughed. 'Poor Lorna hasn't any idea of what you're talking about!' She turned to Lorna and explained, 'Anton is Dutch and he lives and works in Amsterdam. He's an architect, like Michael——'

'Not like Michael,' Eve interrupted. 'Daddy's work is old-fashioned by comparison.'

'Thank you, darling.' Sir Michael was handing the drinks around. 'Your sherry, Lorna. I'm sure you're used to my daughter by now. She's not the most charming of creatures.'

Lorna managed a smile. She was wishing she'd asked for something stronger to drink. As far as everyone else was concerned the atmosphere was lighthearted and warm. But Lorna was an outsider and she felt like an outsider. Added to that she had Anton's scrutiny to contend with, and while she was grateful that he had not said anything to embarrass her further, she wished fervently that he would turn his speculative eyes elsewhere. Worse was the fact that he was watching her with amusement. Perhaps he *was* planning to let the Summers know he'd met Lorna before? Lord, she felt so tense and uncomfortable!

Julian came in then, looking a little worse for wear in spite of the smart suit he was wearing. He kissed all three women in turn and explained to Lorna that he'd had one too many the night before. 'We started the celebrations last night,' he smiled. 'It's going to be quite a week, Lorna. I hope you're feeling fit! I mean, for tonight, tomorrow, the engagement party and then New Year's Eve!'

Lorna wanted to say something about being unsure how long she could stay, but she didn't. She would have to dream up something very plausible if she were to leave The Lions before she was expected to. The last thing she wanted was to hurt her hosts' feelings.

'I'm sure Lorna will cope.' The deep voice brought Lorna's head up with a snap and she found herself thinking once again what a very attractive smile Anton Van der Buren had. 'I intend to look after her personally and to see that she has a memorable week.'

The smile was enigmatic now, and Lorna lowered her eyes. Just what did he mean by that?

'Good for you, Anton!' Sir Michael smiled at him fondly before turning to his future son-in-law. 'What will you have to drink, Julian? A hair of the dog?'

Julian grimaced. 'Tonic water, Michael. Straight.'

'Now where was I?' Lady Summers turned her attention back to Lorna. 'Ah, yes, I was telling you that Anton is an architect. Yes. Well, he's leaving Amsterdam and coming to live in England. My husband is shortly retiring from his company and he wants Anton to take his place as senior partner.'

'And Anton,' put in Sir Michael, 'keeps talking about retiring himself! Which is ridiculous at his age, don't you think?'

Lorna really could not have cared less one way or the other. But she could hardly say that. 'I don't know, Sir Michael. It depends on so many things.' She looked at the man in question, feigning interest for the sake of good manners. 'And how come you want to settle in England?'

'I like England.' The broad shoulders shrugged slightly. 'And Michael is exaggerating grossly. I'm not thinking of retiring, just of taking things a little easier. Let's call it semi-retirement. I'm thinking of working from home—doing private commissions for individuals, that sort of thing.'

'Have you found yourself a house yet, by the way?' Eve asked as she perched herself on Julian's lap.

'I'm working on it,' Anton said quietly, which could have meant anything. Turning to Lorna, he said, 'The question needs a great deal of thought, as you'll appreciate.'

She didn't quite know what he meant until Julian clarified it. 'Absolutely,' he said gravely. 'If you take over Michael's business, there'd be little point in selling up your own concern in Holland. You might just as well make Summers an affiliated company and split your time between London and Amsterdam. You'd end up doing more than you're doing now!'

'Whose side are you on?' Sir Michael admonished. 'I'm trying to sell Anton on the idea, Julian, and here you are trying to put him off! Besides, you're wrong. Anton has already sold out in Holland. He's at a loose end—or will be soon. My belief is that he'll get bored if he's no longer working twelve hours a day. He thrives on work! And can you blame me for wanting to ensure my business is handed over to the best architect in Europe?'

'He's exaggerating again,' Anton said mildly, not in the least put out. He was still addressing his remarks to Lorna, still assuming she was interested.

Strangely enough, she *was* becoming interested. She wondered why a Dutchman with a thriving business in his own country should want to sell up and move to another land and do—what? Private commissions for individuals, he'd said. She assumed that meant he would design houses for people who were rich enough to have their homes built to their own specifications.

'All right, gentlemen, I think that's enough. I didn't mean this to turn into a full-scale discussion!' Lady Summers, an elegant woman with greying fair hair, waved her hand dismissively. 'We're in danger of boring Lorna now!' She smiled, her manner charming and interested as she turned to Lorna, changing the subject. 'Tell us about yourself, dear.'

Lorna groaned inwardly. Here it comes, she thought. Question time. I don't belong here. What am I doing here? 'Oh, there's very little to tell,' she said lightly, noticing at once the cheeky way in which Anton raised an eyebrow at her, his eyes amused and disbelieving.

'Eve's told me all about your shop and how

successful it's becoming. Of course you'll get a lot of tourists in Windsor.' Lady Summers, happily, picked on the one subject Lorna didn't mind talking about.

'Yes. I've been open for just a year now, so I have an idea of what to expect from season to season.'

'Do you live in Windsor?' The question came from Anton.

'Of course she does,' Eve said impatiently. 'I told you Lorna has a flat above the shop.'

Eve had, he remembered now, told him this when he had arrived at The Lions the previous day. It had been then that he had learned of the additional guest the Summers were having for Christmas week. But Anton had paid little attention. How could he have known that the Lorna Stewart he'd been told about would turn out to be Cathy Brenner's sister? No wonder he had been unable to find her in the London telephone directories! He'd been looking for the wrong name in the wrong area.

'I would find it very daunting,' Eve's mother went on, 'buying clothes for a shop. I mean, people's tastes vary so much, don't they? I'm sure I would tend to buy only those things which I liked personally!'

'Luckily, I've never been tempted to do that!' Lorna smiled, pleased because Lady Summers was genuinely interested. 'I mean, I'd never have sold anything to Eve, if I did that!'

'Lorna has superb dress sense,' Julian put in. 'She and Eve argue constantly over what suits Eve, but— well, wait till you see the dress she's wearing for the engagement party!'

'Your aunt's car is coming up the drive,' Sir Michael said then. 'She's only an hour late. Not bad, considering her great age.'

Lady Summers stood up. 'Are both the children with her?'

'Looks like it.'

Sir Michael and his wife left the drawing room and Lorna took the opportunity of escaping for a few minutes. She wanted a few minutes' privacy, time to collect herself, before meeting more new people. 'I—think I'll freshen up before we eat,' she said casually. 'If you'll show me to my room, Eve.' She excused herself to the men and went upstairs with her friend, knowing a sense of relief immediately she left the company of Anton Van der Buren.

'I'll leave you to it.' Eve opened the door of a guestroom. 'I'll go and say hello to aunt Mary. See you soon, Lorna. Can you find your way back to the drawing room okay?'

'Yes.' Lorna laughed, though it wasn't a silly question. The Lions was a huge house and one could quite easily get lost in it. They had turned several corners before reaching the first floor corridor where Lorna's bedroom was. This was the guest wing, presumably.

Her clothes had been unpacked and hung in the wardrobe, her toiletries placed neatly on a shelf in the adjoining bathroom. Lorna perched on the side of the bath, bewildered by the morning's events. She wanted to go home, but of course, there was no question of her doing that. What possible reason could she give for leaving?

It wasn't like Lorna to be so lacking in confidence, but it had all been too much for her. Firstly, this vast house with its antiques, its rich furnishings, family portraits and its servants—not to mention its titled owners. She felt like a fish out of water.

And meeting Anton Van der Buren had been a tremendous shock. As far as everyone else was concerned, they had never met before. She was grateful to him for saying nothing about their first meeting, but ... of all the people in the world ... fancy being obliged to spend Christmas with him! If Cathy knew about this she would laugh her head off, no doubt.

She sighed, took a long, hard look at herself in the mirror and gave herself a quick pep talk. Lorna prided herself on being able to keep a balance on things, to

keep things in perspective. But sometimes she let herself
down, failed to do that, as she had when she'd
interfered in Cathy's business and gone to tackle Karel
... Anton. Her own bias against men had prompted her
then, even though she was well aware that not all men
were out to serve their own ends. She must stop this
feeling of resentment towards Anton when he had done
nothing whatever to deserve it.

As for staying at The Lions—well, it was only her
own sense of inadequacy which would prevent her from
enjoying herself. She had always felt at ease with Eve
and Julian, and Sir Michael and Lady Summers were
friendly, charming people. So what was there to feel
tense about? From now on she would just relax and be
herself.

She freshened her lipstick, flicked a comb through
her hair and went downstairs feeling much better in
herself.

The drawing room was buzzing with conversation.
The 'children' who had arrived with Aunt Mary were
brother and sister and about the same age as Lorna.

'Ah, Lorna, there you are!' Sir Michael came over to
her at once. 'Come and meet my niece and nephew.
Cassandra and Roger are two very talented people,
albeit in different directions. Cassie works for me. She's
fresh from university and she thinks she knows it all.
Still, Anton will quickly disabuse her of that idea when
she finds herself working for him!'

All this was said in Cassandra's hearing and she gave
her uncle a controlled smile. She was a very attractive
girl with jet black hair and blue eyes. The white angora
dress she was wearing was perfect for her and showed
off her figure to full advantage.

'You're an architect?' Lorna couldn't keep the
surprise from her voice.

'She will be by the time we've finished with her,' Sir
Michael chuckled.

'It's nice to meet you.' She gave Lorna a rather limp
handshake and glanced over at Anton before making a

retort to her uncle. 'Anton and I would make a very good team, Uncle Michael. I'm trying to convince him of that.'

'Keep trying,' Sir Michael grinned. 'Perhaps you can influence him in ways that I can't! I haven't got your charm.'

'Has he given you his decision yet?'

'No.'

Cassandra's eyes went again to Anton, who was talking to Eve and a white-haired old lady. She was interested in him, Lorna observed, in more than a professional sense.

'I'm Roger Summers.' Cassie's brother introduced himself, bowing and laughing as he took Lorna's hand. 'I'm the black sheep of the family. Talented, perhaps, but as yet undiscovered.'

'And what does that mean?' Lorna took in his jeans, his worse-for-wear leather jacket, his open-necked shirt and the black hair which was far too long. He looked very out of place among these people who had dressed so beautifully for Christmas Day. But he wasn't out of place. He was family, black sheep or no.

'I'm a painter.' Blue eyes, eyes remarkably like his sister's, smiled at her. 'Struggling but optimistic.'

Lorna glanced from him to Cassandra. 'Are you two twins?'

'Yes, more's the pity.' Cassandra looked at him disdainfully. 'He's a scruffy lout, don't you think?'

She didn't wait for Lorna's response, she went over to Anton and linked her arm through his, smiling up at him from a very vivacious face. Of course she hadn't been interested in Lorna's reply. She had dismissed Lorna, and very rudely, too. Lorna summed the girl up in two minutes flat. Cassie Summers was beautiful, sophisticated and talented. But she had an affected, plum-in-the-mouth voice, was self-opinionated and superior. She was also a bitch.

Lorna was introduced to Mrs Collingham, Lady Summers' aunt, and was surprised all over again. She was very thin, very old but as bright as a button. Without realising it, Lorna relaxed completely as Mrs Collingham started chatting to her about anything and everything.

At one o'clock precisely Sir Michael announced that it was time for Christmas dinner and he offered the old lady his arm and led the way to the dining room.

Lorna felt a hand on her shoulder, and stiffened as she turned to see warm brown eyes smiling down at her. 'Miss Stewart,' Anton said formally, with a slight inclination of his head.

Nonplussed, Lorna linked her hand under the arm he was extending and followed Roger and Lady Summers into the dining room. Eve and Julian were behind them, which left Cassandra unescorted and not looking at all pleased about it. She had obviously expected to be accompanied by Anton, and Lorna wished that the man had done what was expected of him. Why had he picked on Lorna? Was this the sort of thing he'd referred to when he'd said he was going to 'look after' her?

The meal was quite unlike any other Christmas celebration Lorna had experienced. It was a banquet, and it went on for more than two hours. She was seated with Mrs Collingham to her left and Roger Summers to her right. Anton was on the other side of the table and was virtually monopolised by Cassandra. When it occurred to Lorna that she was far more aware of Anton than she ought to be, she told herself it was just the aftermath of the shock of meeting him again. And meeting him here, of all places.

But the truth was that she thought him an extremely attractive man. His smile fascinated her. When he wasn't smiling, the brown eyes were watchful, warm, giving the impression of sincerity and openness. But when he laughed they lit up with intensity, crinkling at the corners and making one want to laugh with him.

His rugged features told another story. The nose was straight, the chin square and no-nonsense and his jawline was strong and clearly defined. He had *presence*, and Lorna was not the only one who thought so. Yet he seemed to be a quiet man. Oh, he did his fair share of talking, but his manner was controlled, calm, and quite unlike that of Roger Summers.

Roger was talking at Lorna rather than to her. His main topic of conversation was himself. Not that she minded; he was quite easy to get along with provided he got a few nods and noises every now and then. The afternoon went remarkably smoothly, but Lorna's tension returned as often as it left her.

Early in the evening a light buffet supper was laid out and taken advantage of mainly by the friends and neighbours who had been invited for a Christmas drink. Mrs Collingham, who had gone to her room for a nap during the afternoon, appeared again at about eight o'clock, and she and Lorna chatted together, sitting well away from the general hubbub in the vast drawing room. Pop music was playing quietly from an ornate piece of furniture which looked more like a sideboard than a radiogram, and it was only when the volume suddenly increased that Lorna was interrupted.

'You know what this means, don't you?' It was Roger, waving a piece of mistletoe. His face was slightly flushed though good-looking in a boyish sort of way, and he gave Lorna an exaggerated wink.

'Must you?' The protest came from his great-aunt, or whatever Mrs Collingham was to him. 'Lorna and I are having a lovely chat about the sort of clothes I used to wear in the twenties.'

'In your twenties, Aunt Mary?'

'It's the same thing, you rascal. Now kiss me quick and buzz off.'

Lorna laughed fully and openly, delighted with the old lady's choice of words, delighted because she was as sharp as a razor and tickled pink because she knew very well the mistletoe had not been intended as an excuse to kiss *her*. It served very nicely to deflate Roger's buoyancy somewhat.

'But, aunt Mary, I wasn't . . . How about a dance, Lorna?'

Lorna agreed only to save his face. He'd had a couple too many, but he was harmless enough. Besides, she wouldn't get through the entire evening without dancing, she realised that. Several of the new people, friends who'd been invited for the evening, were already dancing.

To her embarrassment Roger planted a kiss—a very light kiss—on her lips as their first dance came to an end. It irritated Lorna beyond words, but she managed not to show it. Happily she was being quite successful in keeping things in perspective tonight.

Until Anton Van der Buren came over.

Not for the first time, his nearness made something inside her recoil from him. It had happened in Karel's living room when she had first met him and he had been standing too close for comfort. It was happening again, now, and this time Lorna had no anger to give vent to which would serve to smother her sense of panic. Certainly this sensation, this fear, was not new to her. But it normally happened only when she was in the company of a certain type of man. She knew why it happened. She knew it was illogical. But she didn't know why it happened when Anton Van der Buren was standing close to her.

The hand which was about to touch her shoulder went instead to the pocket of his slacks and Lorna realised from this that she had let her emotions show on her face. Roger was oblivious, slapping Anton on the back and protesting that this was not an 'excuse me' dance.

Anton didn't answer him. He was looking carefully into Lorna's eyes, his curiosity about her reflected in the drawing together of his brows.

Feeling ill at ease at the way she had frozen him with a single glance, Lorna tried to laugh it off. 'Hello, Anton! If you're about to ask me to dance, the answer has to be no, I'm afraid. I'm still feeling the effects of the wine, and it's getting too hot in here. Perhaps later?'

'By all means—later.' He inclined his head towards her, then glanced in the direction of Mrs Collingham. 'Mary's been trying to catch your attention.'

'Oh! Er—thank you.' She excused herself and crossed the room, forcing herself to walk slowly. So that was what he'd wanted to say to her; he hadn't been about to ask her to dance! She felt stupid, more so as she realised she had asked him to dance later on. She had done that only to make up for her silly behaviour and so she wouldn't have to refuse him in front of someone else. Heavens, he really must think her a very strange person. Maybe she was a very strange person. Not that it mattered—either way.

'I'm sorry to interrupt your fun, Lorna,' Mrs Collingham apologised. 'But Eve seems to have vanished and I don't want to take Emma away from her guests. So would you be kind enough to see me to my room? I'm a little shaky on the stairs these days. Would you mind, dear?'

'Not at all.' Lorna helped her to her feet, glancing at her watch as she did so. 'But it's only—Oh, it's turned eleven! I didn't realise it was that late.'

'Way past my bedtime,' the old lady smiled. 'But you'll come down again and dance till dawn! Quite right, too.'

Not likely, Lorna thought. She was pleased it had turned eleven. It was late enough, just about, for her to escape to her room, too. She wanted to do that very much, far more than she wanted to stay at the party and make small talk or to dance with Anton Van der Buren.

Mrs Collingham's room was on the other side of the house from where Lorna's room was. She bade the old lady goodnight and came back down the sweeping staircase with the intention of telling Sir Michael, and only Sir Michael, that she was going to call it a night. It was Eve she saw first, however. She was opening doors off the main hall, obviously looking for someone.

'Hi, Lorna! It's a good party, isn't it? I've lost Julian, have you seen him?'

'No. Maybe he's outside getting some air,' Lorna grinned. 'Remember that he started the day with something of a handicap!'

'Mmm!' Eve shoved her hair behind her ears, grinning. 'It's been an interesting day, hasn't it?'

'It's been a lovely day, Eve. Thank you.'

Eve looked heavenward. 'You're going to pretend you don't know what I'm talking about, aren't you?'

'There's no need to pretend. What are you talking about?'

'Anton, of course. He's very, very attractive, isn't he?' She laughed outrageously, poking Lorna in the ribs. 'Go on, tell me you haven't noticed.'

'I've noticed,' Lorna admitted. 'So what?'

'So he's interested in you, too. I saw the looks that passed between you when you were first introduced. He fancies you.'

'You're quite wrong.' Lorna laughed in an effort to keep the seriousness from her voice. She couldn't blame Eve for misinterpreting those looks, yet she had to disillusion her. 'So don't go making something out of nothing. Anyhow, I was just going to tell your father I'm on my way to bed——'

'What? You're joking. It's far too early for that!'

'You must forgive me, but I'm shattered. I had a really hard day yesterday and I got up very early today.'

Eve considered for a moment. 'Well, all right. But just this once. No dropping out early from our other parties! Okay?'

'Okay. Tell your mum and dad goodnight and thank you.'

'Anton will be disappointed . . .' Eve teased.

'I'm sure Cassandra will keep him company.'

'You can bet on it.' Eve was quite serious now. 'Look, don't go to bed yet. Don't leave the field wide open for Cassie, she's not one to miss an opportunity.

You might be making a mistake, if you are interested in ——'

'I'm not.' Lorna was equally serious. 'Honestly, Eve, I'm not in the least interested in Anton. Your cousin is welcome to him. Cassie, or anyone else. Goodnight.' Lorna turned around and went back up the stairs, but not before she had noticed Eve's look of puzzlement. Poor Eve. If only she knew about Lorna's first meeting with her father's friend!

The music from the drawing room did not reach Lorna's bedroom and she was glad of the silence. Parties held no novelty for her, which was surprising considering how few she had been to in her life. She drew the curtains against the frosty darkness of the night and had a long, relaxing soak in the bath. She had exaggerated her tiredness to Eve; she had wanted to escape because she'd had enough for one day. She would read for a while.

When someone knocked on her door, she was doing just that. Her first thought was not to respond. Then she realised who it would be and she slipped out of bed and pulled on the green silk dressing gown she had brought with her. If anyone had told her earlier that she would invite Anton Van der Buren—or any man—into her room at midnight, she would never have believed it. Yet she was about to do just that.

'I think it's high time we had a chat, don't you?' Anton's gaze did not leave her eyes as she opened the door widely. If he was surprised at this, at the way she readily motioned him inside, he didn't show it.

'High time. Please sit down.' There were two comfortable armchairs in the room and Lorna seated herself opposite him.

'I've been wanting to have a word with you all day,' he said quietly, 'but we haven't had a moment's privacy.'

'Quite. And I've been wanting to thank you for—for not saying anything about our having met before. I mean, the circumstances——'

'It wouldn't have occurred to me to do that.' He smiled. 'Especially as your discomfiture was obvious to me. You've had an unpleasant day, Lorna, and I hope it isn't wholly due to my presence.'

She didn't know how to answer him, she was so surprised. No, her tension throughout the day had not been wholly due to his presence. After the first hour or so she had stopped feeling embarrassed, she had stopped worrying about whether Anton was going to say something to the Summers, because she'd realised he was not. But how shrewd of him to realise that the rest of the day had been quite a strain for her. She hoped nobody else was aware of it.

In the face of her silence, he went on, 'You have the sort of eyes which speak on your behalf, don't you know that?'

'No. And I'm sure you're exaggerating! You've made an accurate guess—or you're particularly good at reading people. I don't know which.' Lorna found herself genuinely amused. More surprising was the ease with which she could talk to him, especially in view of her earlier panic when he'd come up to her in the drawing room.

But she felt safe with him despite their being alone in her bedroom. She felt safe firstly because she knew he was not interested in her personally and secondly because she had reached the conclusion that Anton was a gentleman, a thorough gentleman. He could have made her look foolish in front of Roger, when she'd thought he was going to ask her to dance. But he hadn't. Nor had he said anything to add to her discomfiture when they had been introduced that morning.

As for their meeting in Karel's house . . . 'Why didn't you tell me who you were when we met at Karel's? I mean, I realise what a state I was in, but you could have put me straight before I left.'

His smile was mischievous. 'Left? You mean before you shook the building to its foundations?'

'Whatever.' She laughed without embarrassment at the memory. 'So why didn't you tell me who you were?'

'I tried to. But the situation got out of hand somehow. It got to the point where telling you would have served no useful purpose. Especially since Karel was out of the country.'

Lorna smiled at him. At some level of her mind she had known at their first meeting that this man was not the womanising fashion photographer she was seeking. She had known he fitted neither the image Cathy had built up nor the surroundings, horrid surroundings, in which they had met. She should have listened to her instincts. The trouble was that she had been in too much of a fury to listen to anything—including Anton.

She was paying attention to her inner voice now, however. 'So your silence was a kindness. You didn't want to add to my frustration by telling me Karel was in Africa. You didn't want to make me feel foolish after the insults I hurled at you.'

Anton continued to make light of it. 'Oh, they weren't too bad—except for the one about my being old enough to be Cathy's father.'

Lorna flinched at that, but Anton held up a silencing hand. 'Don't worry about it. At thirty-six I am, technically, old enough to be the father of a nineteen-year-old! It's a depressing thought!'

Lorna got to her feet. This was the perfect note on which to end the conversation. 'Then let me apologise doubly, for making you feel so old and for the entire episode.'

'There's no need,' he laughed. 'I'm only too pleased that we've cleared the air.' He stood up because she was making it very plain to him that she wanted him to go now.

'You heard what—what happened to Cathy?' she asked as she walked to the door.

'Karel phoned and told me.' He saw the concern in her eyes as she turned to face him. 'Cathy is your half-sister, I take it? The different names——'

'Yes.'

He nodded, and Lorna was suddenly aware, again, of the effect his physical nearness had on her. She mentally talked herself down, rapidly, not wishing to let her panic show again. She did not want to spoil things now she had finally established some sort of relationship with Anton. After all, she was going to be in his company until New Year's Day—and that was a whole week away.

'Well, allow me to offer a word of advice. You obviously worry too much about Cathy. She's not a child. She'll make her own mistakes in life, as we all do.'

Lorna sighed, nodding. 'I've already been told off for interfering.'

'I don't blame you for that. You meant well. You were only trying to protect her. But you are not your brother's keeper, Lorna.'

'You're right.' She shrugged and opened the door. 'Thank you for coming to see me. Goodnight.'

'Actually, I——' Whatever he had been about to say, he thought better of it. He bade her goodnight and left without another word.

Anton crossed the corridor and went into his own room. He flung his jacket on the bed and sprawled out in the armchair. A moment later he got up again and looked for the packet of cigarettes he knew he had somewhere. He needed to think. He needed silence.

She was under his skin. He had thought about her every day since meeting her in October, and it was a rare woman who had that sort of effect on him. The party had become uninteresting when he learned that she had gone to her room. He would not go downstairs again. Parties were not his scene, anyway. He had been to enough of them to last a lifetime. They bored him now.

One changes as one gets older, he acknowledged, smiling as he remembered Michael's comment about his thriving on work. It wasn't true. Not any more. His first job after leaving university in England had been with the Summers partnership. His work was still innovative, but in those days ... well, Michael had kept him in check, fondly telling him he was ahead of his time.

And here he was, now, in a position to take over Summers and run things his way. It was an entertaining idea, but that was all. He had reached the zenith of his profession, had run his own very successful company in his native Holland until, recently, he had handed it over to someone else. He was presently extricating himself from it gradually, acting mainly as a consultant until the company's current commissions were finished. The new work coming in had nothing to do with him, and soon he would be quite free.

Anton knew and loved England as well and as much as he knew and loved Holland. He thought about Lorna, living in Windsor, and smiled at the idea. Part of his education had been at Eton and so he knew Windsor, Eton's twin town, like the back of his hand. His entire education had been given to him in England and what was left of the Van der Buren family was divided between the two countries. He had always intended to return to England, though admittedly he had not anticipated doing this at the age of thirty-six. But then he could not have anticipated the change which was taking place in him, the discontent which had started to grow in him more than a year ago.

Would his return to England be sufficient in itself to quell this feeling or would he, as Michael had suggested, grow bored if he had a much lighter work-load? On hearing of Anton's intention to settle here, Michael had made this entertaining proposition about the takeover of Summers. Certainly the nature of the work Michael's company dealt with would be different from the type of commissions Anton had undertaken in Amsterdam. But for how long would Anton be stimulated by this? How long before the discontent returned?

On the one hand he felt that he wanted his time to be his own. He wanted time for things other than work. He wanted time for living—travelling, perhaps. Perhaps? That was the trouble, for on the other hand he could not say that there was anything specific he particularly wanted to do.

Irritated, he put out his cigarette and kicked off his shoes. This was not like him at all, this feeling that he was not fully in command. Michael wanted an answer early in the New Year. The entire business needed careful thought, and here he was, attempting to give it just that but finding himself completely distracted by thoughts of Lorna Stewart.

They would have an affair, of course. She probably knew that as well as he did. It was on the cards. The attraction was mutual; he had felt it pulling between them several times during the day when their eyes had met and held. He knew the routine. He knew also that he would have to move slowly, bide his time for longer than usual because of the bad start they had got off to.

Had he not had more than his fair share of experience with women, he might have thought her uninterested. Indeed he had been puzzled by her response when he had approached her when she had been dancing with Roger. She had looked as if she wanted to bolt. Yet she had welcomed him when he had gone to talk to her in her room. He had hoped to make better progress with her than he had, though. He hadn't expected the interlude to be so short. Still, they had established a rapport. But again, when he had been standing close to her by the door she had looked at him strangely, had seemed very uncomfortable. No, she had been uncomfortable, and no mistake. He had seen it in her eyes.

Anton laughed softly into the stillness of the room. What gorgeous eyes she had! They were so clear, so green, so expressive and made seductive by the thick long lashes surrounding them and that way she had of lowering them when she looked away, breaking contact with his own. She was altogether beautiful, fascinating. She carried herself well, with dignity, and that subtle sway of her hips, the graceful way she sat and crossed one long, shapely leg over another would turn any man's head. Indeed, he had watched heads turning tonight.

Delightful! And he didn't mind at all that she was under his skin. Her hot-and-cold attitude was merely part of an amusing game some women liked to play. And why not? He liked such displays of femininity, he enjoyed the fun of the chase. Considering their first encounter and the shock of meeting here so unexpectedly, he could hardly expect her to be more responsive. There was her pride to consider, and she might be classifying him the way she classified Karel— as some kind of playboy. Anton laughed at the thought. Appreciative of the fairer sex he certainly was. But a playboy he was not!

He looked forward to the weeks ahead. No, to the months ahead. Maybe this affair would last for a year? Or more? It would be slow to start, he knew, but he had a strong feeling that the intriguing Miss Stewart was going to be in his life for quite some time.

CHAPTER FIVE

AT nine the following morning, Lorna came in from her walk around the grounds of the house, took her coat upstairs, then made her way to the breakfast room. Roger and Eve were there, eating bacon and egg and chatting away.

'Good morning, both. Is there some tea in that pot?'

'Good morning, Lorna,' Eve smiled. 'Yes, the pot's full. It's just been made. Do help yourself. Breakfast will be a bit staggered today—heaven knows what time everyone else will come down—so I'll ring for the maid and you can tell her what you'd like to eat.'

'No, no, don't bother. I don't eat breakfast—just tea.'

Roger was shaking his head. 'I might have known.'

'What? That I don't eat breakfast?'

'No!' His boyish face creased with laughter. He had to be about Lorna's age, but he certainly didn't look twenty-five. Or was it that his twin sister appeared older than she was? Perhaps her super sophistication was responsible for that.

'Well, don't keep us guessing,' Eve prompted. 'What might you have known?'

'That Lorna would be one of those women who look just as good first thing in the morning as they do at any other time.' His eyes swept over her appreciatively, taking in the soft blue dress which fitted her to perfection.

'It is Boxing Day, Roger.' Cassandra, obviously having heard her brother's remark, came in and joined them. 'Some of us make the effort to look decent, you know. Just because you're an artist it doesn't give you licence to dress like a layabout.'

'I am a layabout. Good morning, darling.'

Cassandra didn't bother to bid anyone good morning. She poured herself some tea and continued to needle her brother. 'And why the hell are you bothering to flirt with Lorna? I'm sure you're not her type. You haven't got a hope.'

This wasn't called for. Everyone knew that but Cassie. Roger took not the slightest notice of her, however. 'Oh, I don't know. I'm an optimist, remember?' He turned to Lorna then. 'Do you like optimists?'

'Surely everyone loves an optimist?' She kept her tone light. If Roger had been flirting with her, which she doubted, she didn't want to encourage him. Nor did she want to put him down in front of Cassandra, whose opinion of him was already obviously low.

'My friend, the diplomat.' Eve giggled. 'Take no notice of these two, Lorna, they can be boring in the extreme when they pick on each other.'

Cassandra grunted. Then, for the first time since they had been introduced the previous day, her cool blue eyes surveyed Lorna with genuine interest. 'What happened to you last night? You went to bed very early.'

Anton appeared before Lorna had a chance to answer. On seeing him she felt a sensation of ... something she couldn't put a name to. Perhaps it was just that his presence dominated the room. His hair had obviously just been washed and was a darker blond for its dampness. The grey that mingled with it was mainly at the temples and added a touch of distinction. He was dressed casually this morning in a black cashmere sweater and black slacks which were perfectly cut, not too tight but showing plainly the shape of powerful thighs as he walked.

All eyes turned towards him as he bade them good morning. Cassandra's attitude changed at once. Oh, it changed subtly, and Anton wasn't to know it had changed at all, but it confirmed for Lorna that which she already knew. Cassie wanted him to be more than a colleague to her.

'Anton, good morning!' Cassie motioned him to sit beside her. 'You've arrived at the right moment. We're having an interesting conversation. Roger and I were just speculating as to what type of man appeals to Lorna.'

'Why speculate?' he asked, not taking his eyes from Cassie's. 'Why not ask her?'

'I've tried that——' Eve began, but Roger talked over her.

'What fun would that be?' he protested. 'Besides, I might be left without any hope at all. My ego's already taken a blow!'

'It has?' Lorna wondered what she'd said wrong. Not that she took him seriously.

'Of course. You deserted me last night and we'd only been dancing ten minutes or so.'

'That was nothing personal,' Lorna smiled. 'I was tired. I took Mrs Collingham upstairs and decided I'd call it a day, too.'

'And you, Anton?' Cassandra gave him a very effective little-girl-lost look. 'What's your excuse for vanishing so early?'

'It was midnight, Cassie. Not so early.' He smiled at her and Lorna watched the interplay with interest. She looked up to find Eve watching her, amusement dancing in her eyes.

Lorna gave her a quick, hard look, and Eve burst out laughing. What the devil was Eve thinking now? Was she still convinced that Lorna was interested in Anton? She was wrong, if that was what she was thinking.

'Are you going to let us all in on the joke?' Anton asked, 'or is it private? And what does one have to do to get breakfast around here?'

'It's private. And you know the drill. Ring for Pamela and tell her what you want to eat.'

Anton did just that. 'What's happened to your fiancé, Eve? This is the second morning he's slept late. I should get rid of him if I were you.'

'I'd rather go upstairs and join him,' Eve said bluntly:

'Considering you spent most of the night in his room, no doubt, I don't see why you shouldn't.' The remark came from Cassie and it irritated Eve.

She repeated some of her cousin's words. 'No doubt, you say? Which means, of course, that you do have a doubt. Did I or did I not spend most of the night with Julian? Your parents might not mind that sort of thing, but mine would—and well you know it!'

'I don't know about that. They're not as stuffy as you seem to think. You're thirty years old, for heaven's sake, you're not their little girl any more. You don't suppose they don't know that Julian spends half of his nights at your house in Windsor—and that you spend the other half of the week at his flat? Come off it!'

'They don't *know* one way or the other. Which is precisely my point, you ass.'

'Happy families!' Roger said loudly, effectively breaking things up. 'You must find the Summers family either crazy or boring, Lorna. Which is it?'

'Plead the Fifth Amendment,' Anton advised her. 'Don't answer that one.'

Lorna didn't know what he meant, but she had no intention of answering. She was entertained, actually, and content not to join in the conversation. She had never known a proper family life; she had no relatives other than Cathy. These people, all of them, were from a different world, a different culture.

'By the way,' Anton turned to Roger, 'where are your parents? How come they're not here for Christmas?'

'They're in Florida. Staying with Ann, of course. The baby's due any minute.'

'Really? How time flies!'

'Ann is my younger sister,' Roger told Lorna. 'She married an American just over a year ago and settled in Florida.'

Lorna's eyebrows rose as the maid came in with Anton's breakfast. It was big enough to see him through the entire day, but no doubt it wouldn't. Still, there was a lot of him to feed, she thought with amusement. He was a big man, but there wasn't an ounce of excess weight on him. She found herself wondering what he did to keep so fit.

The banter between the Summers continued, and it was not unpleasant; it was tempered nicely with laughter and leg-pulling, then it turned serious when the topic changed to politics. Lorna found herself wondering how the rest of the day was to be spent. She had been told it was open house again this evening, that more friends would be coming for drinks—which meant there would be another party.

'You're very quiet, Lorna,' Anton said suddenly, leaning towards her so he wouldn't be overheard. 'Are you all right? Or is this all a bit much for you at such an early hour?'

'I'm fine, thank you, though I have to admit I'm not at my best first thing in the morning.'

There was that fascinating smile, his eyes denying what she'd just told him. He was a charming man, there was no doubt about it.

Cassandra had heard the exchange. She looked at Lorna apologetically, her voice and her manner soft as she spoke, but for some unknown reason it set Lorna's teeth on edge. 'I must apologise. We're always like this when we all get together, which isn't often, thank heavens.' Very graciously, she asked Lorna what her own family was doing over Christmas. 'Are they abroad? So many people tend to go sun-seeking over Christmas these days, don't they? But I suppose your business keeps you at home?'

'Yes, it does. But my sister is the only family I have. And you've guessed right—she's abroad at the moment.'

'You know, I've been trying to place your accent,' Cassie said lightly, her cool blue eyes raking over Lorna. 'What part of England do you come from, exactly?'

'Scotland.' Lorna said it equally lightly. She wasn't looking at Anton, yet she was aware of his grin.

Cassie reacted with a smile which did not reach her eyes. 'Surely not? You were born in Scotland, I take it. But you didn't spend much time there, did you? I would have recognised the dialect. Where else have you lived? In England, I mean.'

'Oh, here and there. In several counties. You're right again, I moved around quite a bit in my childhood.'

'Your father was in the forces or something, was he? Moving to different bases? Your parents weren't shopkeepers then, like yourself?'

'No, they weren't.' Lorna matched her tone as well as her pleasant smile. On the face of it, Cassandra's questions were natural enough. On the face of it, she was acting as hostess in her aunt's absence—or showing the general interest one person shows to another when they are getting acquainted. Yet Lorna had the distinct feeling that she was under attack. Or was she just being paranoid because she didn't fit in?

'I sometimes wish I'd decided on a simpler way of earning a living,' Cassie went on. 'Architecture can be a very demanding profession at times, though I love it, of course.' She put her hand on Anton's arm. 'You and I would make a very good team, Anton. Now about Summers and Van der Buren—have you made your decision yet?'

'Perhaps Anton would prefer to call it Van der Buren and Summers?' Roger put in.

'When I've made my decision,' Anton said mildly, 'I can assure you you'll be the second person to know about it, Cassie.'

She smiled at him before turning her attention back to Lorna. 'I must tell you something interesting. Strange, really. My father is a barrister—Philip Summers, Q.C.—you'll have heard of him, of course. Eve here took up law as a profession, as you know. And I've taken after her father and find my talents lie in architecture! Isn't that odd?'

'I suppose so,' Lorna smiled.

'Was your father a professional man? Are we likely to know of him?'

'I doubt it.' One thing Lorna no longer doubted was that she was under attack, though why, she didn't know. In the face of such blatant snobbery, she couldn't help reacting. She wasn't angry, she was past caring. Quietly and calmly she said, 'My father was a bricklayer. He died in an accident on a building site before I was born. I didn't know him myself, you see, so I doubt whether your family will know of him.'

In the momentary silence from Cassandra, there was laughter from Roger and Eve looked at Lorna with a mixture of admiration and respect. Anton remained impassive and said nothing.

'Oh! I—I'm sorry,' Cassie looked positively uncomfortable. 'How awful for your mother! They can't have been married long, I suppose.'

It wasn't another attack, because Cassie could not possibly have anticipated the answer, but Lorna took the opportunity of shutting her up good and proper. 'Oh, they weren't married at all,' she said casually. 'They were living together. Mum was five months pregnant when Dad died. She told me they were due to get married on the Saturday, but my father was killed on the Wednesday.'

Cassie didn't know where to look. 'How—how awful for you! I am sorry.'

'Being a bastard? Not at all.' Lorna smiled, her eyes full of mischief. 'You can survive without a father, Cassie. They say you don't miss what you've never had, don't they?' She became aware of her own heartbeat. Inwardly, she was more wound up than she had realised. She bit her tongue, resisting the temptation to say anything else, knowing she would only regret it later.

Anton drained his coffee cup and pushed his plate aside. 'Delicious. Now, Lorna, how about that walk you promised me?'

Lorna felt a rush of gratitude towards him, and she

was aware of Cassandra's eyes upon her. 'Fine.'

'Sorry,' Anton said to everyone in general. 'Nobody else is invited. This is a date.'

'I see,' Cassie said stiffly. 'And when did you make this date?'

'Last night.' Anton got to his feet and held out his hand to Lorna.

She put her hand in his as she stood. 'Anton promised to show me the grounds,' she smiled. Happily, nobody else was aware that she had already been for a walk.

'Have fun.' Eve looked delighted, giving Lorna a broad wink which nobody else could see as Anton held the door open for her.

They went upstairs for their coats and Lorna discovered that Anton's room was directly opposite her own. 'I—didn't realise you were sleeping in there.'

He shrugged. 'Does it worry you?'

'Is there any reason why it should?'

'No.'

'Then it doesn't.'

They went outdoors, Lorna wearing a camel coat and Anton wearing a three-quarter-length sheepskin which was expensive and just the sort of thing she would have imagined him wearing on a cold winter's day. They walked in the direction of the woods at the far end of the grounds, saying nothing for a while.

'I've already seen the grounds,' Lorna said at length.

'I know,' he smiled. 'I saw you this morning from my bedroom window.'

They exchanged looks and Anton took hold of her hand and linked it through his arm. Lorna didn't resist, she just registered her own surprise and pleasure that her arm felt comfortable resting on his. 'It's time to thank you again, Anton. I've come to the conclusion that you're a kind sort of man. Thanks for aiding my escape.'

'It was partly for my own sake,' he admitted. 'I wanted to be alone with you. I want to talk to you. But you were getting very angry with Cassie, and that scene could have developed into something quite nasty.'

'I know. And I'd have been the first to regret it.'

'Even though she instigated it,' he finished.

She laughed suddenly. 'Were you reading my eyes again?'

'Ah, it was easy today. I've seen them angry before, remember?'

They lapsed into silence. Lorna wasn't even curious about what he had to say to her. Basically, she knew, the two of them had nothing of importance to say to one another. She and Anton Van der Buren were worlds apart, and when this week was over they would go back to their respective worlds. But for the moment he was easy to be with, very much so, and nobody was more surprised than she to find herself thinking like this. It came as quite a shock to her, all things considered. Like the fact that he was a man, for instance.

After a long, comfortable silence during which they walked slowly along the path skirting the woods, Anton looked down at her. 'Tell me about yourself, Lorna.' He saw immediately her look of irritation. 'Hey, take it easy! I'm genuinely interested. I'm not doing a Cassie.'

Lorna found herself apologising. 'No, I know. I—it's just . . . you must think me very strange.'

'Yes,' he admitted, smiling. 'But intriguingly so.'

She sighed. 'What the hell am I doing here? At The Lions, I mean. I want to go home, if the truth is known. Right now. To think I could be there in an hour or so . . .'

'Now that isn't very flattering! Think of Eve, at least!'

'Sorry,' she grinned. 'I am thinking of Eve, and her parents. They're lovely people and it was kind of them to invite me. But I feel like a fish out of water.'

'If it's any consolation, I feel a bit like that myself,' he confessed.

'You?' Lorna was astonished. 'But you—you've

known the Summers all your life from what I can gather.'

'Not all my life. Michael gave me my first job when I left university, and we've been fast friends ever since. I think he sort of looks on me as the son he never had.'

'You went to university in England?'

'Cambridge.'

'That's probably why you speak the language so well.'

'I do? Thank you, ma'am. Anyhow, I'm here partly for business reasons, partly out of some inexplicable sense of duty because I was invited to spend Christmas. But between you and me, I'd rather be elsewhere.'

'I—see. An ungracious pair, aren't we?'

'We're not seen to be. Nobody's being offended, nobody's feelings are being hurt.'

Lorna looked at him for a long moment, curious about him. 'Who are you, Anton?' she asked. 'What are you? What do you like and dislike?'

The warm brown eyes lit up with amusement and pleasure. 'That's exactly what I want you to tell me about yourself,' he said. 'Come on, there's a bench over there. Let's sit down for a while.'

Lorna was happy to do that. She'd had enough walking for one day. 'All right, let's see . . . I'm twenty-five, I'm strictly a career girl. *Feline* is my life and I——'

'*Feline*?'

'That's the name of my shop.'

Anton nodded approvingly. 'It conjures up very nice images. Was it your idea?'

'But of course!'

'Pardon me!' he grinned. 'Carry on.'

'I like driving on motorways but not in town traffic. I like travelling on trains but I get sick in coaches. I like walking in the rain, but not if it's windy at the same time. I like work but not housework. Umm . . . I like reading, but I don't have as much time as I'd like to devote to it. I love the theatre, especially musicals. I like watching old films on telly. I've seen *Casablanca* three times and *The Sound of Music* five. Four of those times were at the cinema. How's that?'

'So you're a romantic?'

She looked at him in disgust. 'Not in the slightest.'

'Then you indulge in escapism.'

'Doesn't everyone from time to time?'

'Yes. Everyone does.'

'Now it's your turn.' Lorna lowered her eyes. It was happening again, that physical awareness of him. She had unlinked her arm from his when they sat, and now, without realising it, she edged away from him slightly.

Anton noticed it, but it didn't detract from his enjoyment. 'Right. Driving—I can take it or leave it. My work is becoming more of a burden than a pleasure. I'm thinking of doing less of it, as you know. I don't know what housework is because I've never done any. I like reading, but I don't have as much time as I'd like to devote to it, though that won't always be the case. I haven't got a television, but that'll change soon, too. I like all kinds of music. I like the theatre and the cinema. I've seen *Casablanca* twice but never *The Sound of Music*. Perhaps you'll take me to see it the next time it's on the circuit. How's that for something in common?'

Lorna threw back her head and laughed. 'Not bad at all! Will you marry me?'

'Today?'

'No, it'll have to be tomorrow, silly. Today's Boxing Day.'

He joined in her laughter. 'I also like——' He stopped because she had also begun a sentence with exactly the same words.

'Go on.' He swept out an arm in invitation.

'I also like a person with a sense of humour.'

'That's just what I was going to say.'

Their laughter died away and Lorna glanced at her watch. 'I suppose we should go back.'

'There's no hurry. As long as we're in good time for lunch.' Anton was quite serious now. 'Lorna, I came to

London last week. I tried to contact you before I came out here. Of course, you weren't listed under Brenner in the London telephone directory.'

'No.'

'I found your sister's number, but there was no reply. I was going to ask her for your home phone number. Karel wasn't at home, either. He must be away. Has he taken Cathy abroad?'

'No, no. They're not together.' She was quite bewildered. 'Why—why did you want to contact me last week? I mean, why contact me at all?'

Very casually he said, 'I thought it would be nice to meet, have dinner and sort things out. The misunderstanding, you know. It's a couple of months since all that. I thought we might even have a laugh about it. Don't misunderstand me when I say that.'

'I won't. It's all right.'

'You can imagine my surprise when you came here. For me, it was a very pleasant surprise.'

Lorna caught her lower lip between her teeth. She would have to think before she responded to all this, but for the moment she was too busy cursing herself for her stupidity. It was a fact of life that she was attractive to men and it was something she could not change. But Lorna was not vain, she didn't assume that every man she met would be interested in her. But Anton was. Why else would he want to take her to dinner? It was obvious to her, now, that his friendliness was not without an ulterior motive. She hadn't considered this before. She honestly had not seen him as a potential problem.

'I'd better tell you a few more things about myself,' she said. 'I'm not interested in having dinner with you. The answer would have been no. Anyhow, Cathy wouldn't have passed on my telephone number to you.' She said it nicely, reasonably, wishing only to make herself clear to him. 'I'm not interested in men, in general.'

He wasn't in the least put out. 'Fair enough,' he

shrugged. 'So I take it there's one in particular? Someone you're quite heavily involved with?'

Lorna simply couldn't help smiling. 'No.' After a bad start and then a very friendly, pleasant follow-up, they were now at cross-purposes again. 'I'm not interested, full stop.'

She saw him considering this, amused at what might be going through his mind.

His frown was fleeting and followed immediately by laughter. 'Very well.' He held up a hand before she could say anything, serious now. 'Your reasons for this are your own, Lorna. It's none of my business. I'll admit to finding you a mystery. But can't we be friends—just friends?'

Lorna was very dubious indeed. She could not deny to herself that she liked him, but . . . 'I see little point in that.'

'Then that's a very sad state of affairs.' The deep voice was quiet, sincere. 'Have you so many friends that you don't need a new one?'

He had managed, somehow, to make her feel ashamed. She was well aware of her cynicism as far as men were concerned. But what was it about this man? Could he mean what he said—that he wanted friendship and nothing else? Should she be flattered instead of doubtful? A man like him, he could have any woman he wanted, and he was surely aware of that.

'Lorna?'

'I—no. I haven't got many friends. It's—I suppose I'm pretty anti-social.'

He couldn't take his eyes from her face. A beautiful girl like this, she had such character, was so easy to talk to, with a delightful sense of humour. Why should she be anti-social? Surely she wasn't really uninterested in men? Yet he had the feeling that she meant what she was saying. Something told him that this was not simply a question of her playing hard to get, not part of the game that was the fun of the chase. He was challenged, more intrigued than ever. Furthermore, he did want to establish a friendship with her. He liked her enormously. 'Have lunch with me tomorrow, Lorna. We'll escape together for a couple of hours.'

'Go out, you mean? How—how could we do that? I thought you said we shouldn't be seen to be ungracious. What would Sir Michael think?'

'Don't worry about that. Tomorrow is nothing special. I've told Michael I have to go out for a while in any case. Come with and then we'll have lunch.'

'No. I—er—thank you, but no.' She stood up. 'Let's go back now. They'll be wondering where we are.'

Anton didn't push it. He took her arm and they walked towards the house. Lorna felt confused, sad. She had refused his invitation when she had really wanted to accept it. She thought it would be pointless to go out with Anton Van der Buren—but on the other hand an uninterrupted day of Cassandra's company did not appeal to her in the least. She scorned herself for thinking that. If only that were the real reason for her ambivalence. Who did she think she was kidding— herself? She was scared of Anton, that was the top and bottom of it.

'What is it you're afraid of, Lorna?'

She stopped in her tracks, knowing full well he could not have read her mind. 'I—don't know what you mean.'

'Is it me?' His face was serious, his eyes troubled. 'Surely it isn't me? I'm offering friendship, that's all. Don't put me down as some kind of Don Juan because of what happened between my cousin and your sister.'

'I'm not,' she said quickly. 'I wouldn't do that.' She meant it. She wouldn't judge Anton by the actions of his cousin any more than she would want him to judge her by Cathy's. She and Cathy were very different people, as were Anton and Karel—if Cathy's original description of the man were to be believed at all.

'All right, then tell me why you're afraid. Tell me why you won't come out with me tomorrow.'

'I'll do better than that—I'll accept. Okay?'

'Okay indeed!'

Nothing else was said. Lorna knew it was ridiculous, her having made such a big deal over a simple invitation to lunch. But there had been a battle going on inside her mind, and she wasn't sure whether she had lost or won that battle by agreeing to go out with Anton.

By the middle of that evening she found herself waiting for an opportunity to speak to Anton alone—to tell him she had changed her mind. But she didn't get a chance to speak to him alone. Fewer people than expected had turned up at The Lions because fog had drifted in in the early evening and by nine o'clock the visibility outside was down to a few yards.

Consequently it was a small party and they ended up drinking and playing Charades. Lorna went to bed at the same time as Mrs Collingham again, and there were no protests from anyone. She was just stripping off her clothes when there was a knock at her door.

'It's Eve! Can I have a word, Lorna?'

Lorna opened the door, smiling. 'You're not going to tell me off for vanishing again, are you?'

'No!' Eve flopped down on the bed. 'Tonight's been a real let-down—thanks to the weather.' She looked apologetic. 'I came to apologise for Cassandra's behaviour this morning. My cousin can be quite a bitch at times.'

'And a snob,' Lorna said bluntly.

'Oh, yes, that, too, I'm afraid. But there was more to it than that, Lorna. I don't think you were aware of it.'

'More to it?' Lorna slipped into her dressing gown. 'What do you mean?'

Eve was obviously uncomfortable, embarrassed. 'She was trying to put you down in front of Anton. Of course she succeeded in doing just the opposite—in my eyes as well as his. You handled her beautifully. I was proud of you.'

'Bless you!' Lorna couldn't help smiling. 'Thanks. But where is all this leading?'

'Look, she fancies Anton like mad—that's obvious. And despite all her faults, she usually gets the men she wants. She's got a boy-friend at the moment and she wouldn't bring him here for the holidays because she knew Anton would be here. You're cramping her style, it's as simple as that. This morning's nastiness was pure jealousy—pure bitch.'

'But why . . .'

'Because she followed Anton from the party last night. She went to his room and he wasn't in there. You'd left an hour or so earlier . . .'

Lorna was aghast. 'She thought Anton was with me?' A blush suffused her cheeks as she suddenly realised that that was precisely where Anton had been.

Fortunately, Eve misunderstood the blush. 'I know, I know. You only met him yesterday, for heaven's sake. And I know you better than that, but——'

'But Cassandra doesn't. She must judge everyone by her own standards. It seems to me she's altogether too interested in who spent last night with whom.'

'I'll second that,' Eve grinned. 'Anyway, she came and told me of her suspicions and I told her to mind her own damned business.'

'Good for you,' Lorna laughed.

Almost sheepishly, Eve added, 'And I'm trying very hard to do the same thing. But I can't help being amused to hear that Anton's taking you to lunch tomorrow, especially in view of your denial of interest.'

Lorna's heart sank. So she was too late to cancel their outing. She hadn't realised Anton had said anything to anyone. She couldn't cancel now and make him, and herself, look foolish. 'Yes, I—I am having lunch with him. But don't you go reading anything into it!'

'Of course not!' Eve's eyes were laughing at her.

'Get out of here,' Lorna grinned. 'And stop teasing me!'

Eve slithered off the bed, laughing her head off. 'I'm not saying a word—except that I don't blame you. And that this is one in the eye for old Cassie!'

'Wait a minute.' Lorna was suddenly serious. 'Has there been something between Cassie and Anton? In the past, I mean?'

'No. They met some years ago, when Anton came over from Holland and spent a week here. Then last October he spent two weeks in London during which he was in Daddy's office most of the time, talking about the business. He took Cassie out to dinner once or twice—but again it was only business.' Eve got as far as the door and then she turned, thoughtful. 'Lorna, Anton asked me something about you just now, and I didn't know the answer.'

'What did he ask?'

'Whether you've been jilted or something in the past. Whether someone hurt you.'

Lorna sighed inwardly but said nothing. It was perfectly understandable he should ask a question like that in view of her behaviour and what she'd said to him.

'Lorna, I'm not prying, but——'

'It's all right—I could never accuse you of prying. The answer is yes, someone did hurt me in the past.'

Eve nodded, making no comment and asking no more questions, 'Goodnight, Lorna.'

Lorna turned the key in the lock and leaned heavily against the bedroom door. Her hands were trembling. All day, or rather since her walk with Anton, Jake Dougan had been in her thoughts. He was the man who had hurt her, though not in the way Eve had meant.

She brushed her teeth and got into bed, too tired to take a bath. Her body was tired, but her mind was too active to permit sleep. For once, she did not try to push Jake from her mind. For once, she allowed herself to think about the distant past, to think about him and about her mother. Perhaps if she went through it again, it would help her to restore her sense of balance, to put things back into perspective.

Her mother, Jean, had been a pretty woman—once. In the few years prior to her death she had looked years older than she actually was. She had been unwell with the sort of illness that could not be seen on X-rays, a mixture of depression and exhaustion. There had always been a man in her life. Though it was beyond Lorna's comprehension, her mother had seemed to need a man and had always attracted the wrong kind. She married Cathy's father when Lorna was five. Prior to that there had been a man living with them for a year or so, but he was very dim in Lorna's memory.

Cathy was born a year after the marriage and the family moved from Glasgow to Sheffield because Thomas Brenner supposedly had a job lined up there. One year later he was sent to prison for burglary, and the first Jean knew of his activities was when the police came to the house and arrested him. Jean had nearly always worked, part-time mostly, as a barmaid and sometimes as a cleaner. She was a fool as far as men were concerned; working when they didn't, or wouldn't, cleaning and cooking for them, crying over them. But she was not foolish enough to hang around and wait for Thomas Brenner's release. She took the girls to live in Newcastle in the hope that he wouldn't trace her.

Then she went out with a couple of men she had met in the pub where she worked. It was in a rough area, both men were out of work and both of them treated her badly, borrowing money, scrounging meals at the house. The later of the two moved in with them, but it only lasted six months.

There followed a period when life wasn't too bad, when there was no man in Jean's life. But when Lorna was ten, her mother met Jake Dougan and they moved to Manchester, where he came from. Jake got and held down a job on the railways and Lorna thought him an improvement on her other 'uncles', though he drank like a fish and spent most of his spare time in the bookmakers'. Much of the time, he ignored Lorna and Cathy, which suited them both.

After a couple of years he was fired from his job and started drinking more heavily. Jean started working lunchtimes as well as evenings as a barmaid, and it was around that time that she started to look ill. It was also around that time that Jake started paying attention to Lorna in a way that frightened her. On the evenings when he didn't go to the pub where Jean worked, he would sit at home and drink. Lorna grew afraid of him, of the way he looked at her, of the way he would suddenly appear when she was undressing for bed or the way he would sometimes get hold of her in a supposedly jovial manner and let his hands roam over her.

She was thirteen when he attacked her. Jean had been in hospital for several weeks with bronchial pneumonia. Every detail of that day and night were stamped indelibly on Lorna's memory. It was the first week of January and she was on school holidays. They were living on the seventh floor of a scruffy block of flats. The rent had not been paid for several weeks and the men from the Council had visited that day. Lorna witnessed the row between them and Jake over the rent and the condition the flat was in. Afterwards, he went out and came home hours later, blind drunk.

Lorna was in bed with Cathy, who was sound asleep. She heard the front door slam, heard Jake stumbling around and then a crash as something in another room was smashed. It was just before midnight; she remembered clearly looking at the clock and then listening hard for another movement from the next room. Jake yelled to her twice, his voice slurred. 'Lorna! Lorna, get in here, you little bitch, and help me.'

She went to him because she was too frightened not to. More than once she had seen him hit her mother when he was drunk, more than once he had thrashed out at her and Cathy, impatient with their childishness. Jake was half sitting, half sprawled on the kitchen floor, one hand streaming with blood and his other hand clutching a broken bottle of whisky. 'Get me a cup or something! *Quick*!'

Understanding that his main concern was to salvage

what was left of his booze, Lorna poured it into a cup and put in on the draining board.

'Wait a minute, you little bastard!' he shouted at her as she was about to go back to bed. 'Help me up. Get me something to wrap around this.' He stuck his hand under the cold water tap, his eyes closing against the pain which must have sobered him a little, though he was swaying on his feet.

Now, Lorna closed her eyes, remembering how she had told him so innocently that they had no bandages. If she had used her brains, if she had just slipped back into the bedroom and fetched a pillowcase or something she could have cut into a bandage, maybe the scene would have ended there. And maybe not.

She shuddered, thinking it curious that she should remember sounds and smells as strongly as she remembered Jake touching her, as strongly as she remembered the visual horror of it. But she did. First there was the sound of her nightie tearing as Jake got hold of it by the neck and ripped it from her. Then there was the sight of the blood from his hand, smeared on her chest in a long line. She remembered the look in his eyes as he took in the sight of her young, budding breasts. And his laughter—raucous, horrible, drunken.

He lifted her bodily, cursing when she screamed as hard as her lungs would allow, her arms beating against him, her legs kicking out wildly. There was a dark patch then, where her memory was incomplete because he slapped her so hard that she was stunned into momentary blackness. She was thrown on to the sofa, naked and petrified at the realisation of his intention. Jake kneeled at the side of her, one hand raised as he threatened her not to make a sound, his other hand forcing its way between her legs, his fingers pushing and probing, scratching and hurting her beyond endurance.

He stank of whisky, on his breath and on his clothes, and when she screamed again he silenced her by covering her mouth with his own. The stench of his breath was one of her most vivid memories. That, the blood which kept pouring from his hand and the blood he drew from her right breast as he sank his teeth around the nipple.

She remembered how his hair had looked as he did this to her; it was thin hair, ginger and very greasy. How old would he have been—forty, perhaps? Forty-five? To one of thirteen years he seemed old; to a slender girl he seemed like the strongest man on earth. He was in fact slight and of medium height, possessed of a wiry strength she would never have believed he had.

He didn't rape her—technically. He didn't even get close to it. But he mauled her abominably and several times he hit her with the belt he'd removed from his trousers, in an effort to silence her. And throughout all this he was cursing Jean, muttering something about it all being her fault, something about the bitch being ill.

Lorna would not be silenced. She screamed and fought with everything she had in her, and it was Jake's own drunkenness that spared her. That, and Cathy.

Nobody else came to her aid. Where they lived, screams and rows were not sufficiently unusual to bring neighbours rushing to one's aid. But Cathy came into the room, seven years old and crying, screaming at the top of her voice. 'Stop it! *Stop it!* Jake! Don't hurt her, Jake! *Jake!*'

She was enough of a distraction. It gave Lorna a few seconds in which to act as he pulled away from her. One thing she could not remember was what she hit him with, but it was something heavy, something she grabbed from a low table nearby. She struck him on the side of the head. It was only a glancing blow and if he had not had so much to drink, it might not have sent him sprawling to the floor.

Her last memory of Jake was of him vomiting as he tried to get up, his trousers hanging loosely around his thighs, him saying, 'Wait a minute . . . Wait a minute . . .' as Lorna bolted from the room. The neighbours had not come to her, but they did take her and Cathy in for the night when she went to them.

Feeling hot, disturbed, Lorna got out of bed now and opened a window, only to close it again immediately. She had forgotten about the fog. On her breast, on the edge of the delicate skin surrounding the nipple, she still bore a small scar which was the mark of Jake's teeth tearing her flesh.

Yes, she had been hurt in the past.

But the past was past and she tried very hard to keep it in perspective. Of course she would never forget Jake's attack, but she tried not to let it colour her view of men in general. That, or anything else in her past. She failed sometimes, though, as she had when she'd placed the blame for Cathy's pregnancy wholly on Karel and had gone storming round to his house. Still, she did *try* to keep a balanced view.

Tonight's thinking, however, did nothing to help her understand her mixed feelings as far as Anton Van der Buren was concerned. In no way at all did Anton remind her of Jake. So why did she experience this sense of panic from time to time when she was with him? That usually happened to her only when she found herself confronted with a man who bore a striking resemblance to her attacker—which was rare.

She simply could not understand why there were moments when she felt afraid of Anton, especially since she knew him to be a gentleman. He could not be compared in *any* way with Jake Dougan, so why did it happen?

CHAPTER SIX

'A HOUSE? Oh! You didn't say.' They were in Anton's car, just turning out of the drive at The Lions. It was a big car, a Volvo, big and solid—like the man who was driving it. He had mentioned that he had to go out today in any case—whether Lorna joined him for lunch or not—but he hadn't said he wanted to view a house.

'Do you mind, Lorna? It'll only take half an hour or so.'

'Not at all! I love looking at houses!'

He smiled at her enthusiasm. 'You do?'

'Well, I usually only get to look at big houses from the outside, of course.'

'And what makes you think I'm looking for a big house?'

She was stumped. 'I don't know. Isn't it?'

Anton put his foot down as the road straightened ahead of them. 'Compared to Michael's place it'll be a shack, I'm sure. It's on the Hampshire/Surrey border. I haven't got a photograph, estate agents' details or anything, because the owners are selling privately. They gave me details over the phone last week and I made an appointment for today.'

When they got on to the main road he accelerated further and Lorna relaxed completely as the heating came on full strength. It was a bitterly cold day but surprisingly clear after last night's fog. 'What kind of place are you looking for? Have you got a definite picture in your mind?'

'No. If that were the case I'd design my own home, buy the land and have it built. What I have in mind is a feeling rather than a mental picture. Put it this way, I'll know the right place when I see it.'

A feeling . . . She knew exactly what he meant. 'And what if you don't find the right place?'

'Then I'll have to invent it.'

'And put in the atmosphere—the feeling—yourself.'

'Precisely.'

'Are you looking specifically in the area you mentioned?'

'No.' He glanced at her, his brown eyes smiling. 'Anywhere within a fifty-mile radius of London will do.'

'Within commuting distance, eh? Does this mean you've decided to take over Summers'?'

'No. It means I want to live in the country but be reasonably near the metropolis. I'm not going to take over Michael's company. That's what he and I were discussing together in the library this morning.'

It was also the reason Cassandra had gone back to London, no doubt. It was either that or because she couldn't stand the attention Anton was giving to Lorna. Maybe it was a mixture of both. Cassandra would be back for the engagement party, though—not that Lorna cared particularly one way or the other. She had used her wish to escape from Cassandra and her snooty attitude, her probing questions, as the reason for accepting this invitation from Anton. Now, however, she faced the fact that she found Anton's company a pleasure, and he had also been very persuasive in getting her to agree to this outing, somehow managing to make her feel unreasonable when she had initially refused. All in all she was very confused about the effect this man had on her. And that bothered her.

'Have you no comment to make, Lorna?'

'About what?'

'The fact that I shall have a lot of time to spare when I move to England. The fact that I've decided against the takeover.'

She shrugged. 'It will hardly affect me one way or the other.'

'Ah,' he smiled, 'but if I'm living within fifty miles of London, at no point will I be too far away to drive over to Windsor and take my new friend out.'

'You have a friend in . . . Oh, do you mean me?'

When he gave her that roguish smile, she decided there and then it was time to put him straight. 'Look, Anton, when this week is over, we shan't be seeing each other again. You'll go back to your world and I'll go back to mine. I've told you, I'm not interested. I wish you'd believe that.'

He slowed the car and swung it off the main road, turning to her as he straightened up again, a blank look on his face. 'I'm sorry, I didn't hear what you said. I was too busy looking for the turning.'

Lorna just stared at him, determined not to show her amusement at his blatant, outrageous lie.

They turned on to a gravel driveway which had perfectly neat gardens flanking either side of it. 'No-o-o, I don't think so,' Anton drawled. 'Still, we'll have a look inside—more as a matter of courtesy than for any other reason. It won't take long.'

'Is this the first house you've looked at?'

'No.' He shrugged. 'I'm afraid that this will be the seventh.' He had just rung the doorbell when, as if from nowhere, an Old English Sheepdog came bounding towards them, barking its head off.

Lorna turned, smiling and not in the least perturbed. 'Well! Who are you?'

The dog promptly stopped and cocked its head to one side, looking up at her. Then he greeted her by standing on his hind legs and plonking two great muddy paws on her immaculate camel coat.

The woman who had answered the door was horrified, apologising profusely. 'Oh, I'm so sorry. I wondered where he'd got to. He must have got out the back door.' She looked from Lorna to Anton and back again. 'I'm terribly sorry, Mrs Van der Buren . . .'

Her assumption fazed Lorna far more than the dog had done. She looked expectantly at Anton, waiting for him to put the woman right, but he just quirked an eyebrow at her and grinned.

They didn't bother viewing the upper floor. It was a

big house, in fact—by Lorna's standards at any rate. Two sniffling children trailed behind as the lady of the house showed them the downstairs rooms. Politely, Anton told her they would look no further. 'It's a charming house, but it's really not what we're looking for.'

They were back in the car within ten minutes and the first thing Anton did was to take hold of Lorna's hand. She tried to snatch it away, but he held on tightly.

'What did you say that for?' she protested. 'It's not what *we're* looking for!'

'And why did you take your gloves off? Did her assumption bother you so much that you had to let her see you weren't wearing a wedding ring?'

'Yes,' she said sullenly.

'Your eyes are sparkling . . .'

'May I have my hand back, please?'

He raised her hand to his lips, just as he had when they had been introduced officially. 'How come you're angry with me but you didn't get angry with that dog?'

'I like dogs.'

'Oh, Lorna!' He laughed so heartily that she couldn't help joining in. Even more amusing was that she hadn't actually meant what he had inferred from her remark. Well, not quite.

'You certainly know how to make a man feel good!' He sobered as he caught sight of her coat. 'What do we do about that?'

'Nothing. It's only mud. We—*I*—just let it dry and then it'll brush off.'

They had a super lunch in a very nice hotel, quite a small hotel, about twenty minutes' drive from the house they'd viewed. Afterwards, they took coffee and brandy in the cosy bar in which a huge coal fire was burning. For the first time in more than two hours there was silence between them. A comfortable silence. Lorna was looking into the fire, enjoying it because it was a rare sight these days—a coal fire.

She was perfectly at ease, replete and just a little

sleepy. 'I can see faces in the——' She broke off as she looked up to find Anton watching her, an expression on his face quite unlike anything she had seen before. She wondered what it meant. 'Is something wrong, Anton?'

Almost inaudibly he said, 'No.' Then more firmly, 'No, nothing at all. You can see faces in the coals?'

'Mmm.'

'I've got a couple of dogs.'

'What?' She blinked, not following him.

'Sorry,' he smiled. 'I'd moved on to the next thought. You said earlier that you like dogs. I've got a couple of German Shepherds.'

'Oh, I like Alsatians! I've never had one of my own, of course. But they'll have to go into quarantine, won't they? When you bring them over here? You will bring them to England?'

'Certainly. They're already in quarantine.' He signalled the waiter as he drained his glass. 'Another brandy, Lorna? That house was pretty chaotic, wasn't it? Of course, one has to look beyond that. How do you feel about children?'

Lorna held up her hands as if in protest, her laughter tinkling. 'Wait a minute, let me guess ... Are we playing some kind of word game? Or is this Twenty Questions? Or are you hopping from one train of thought to the next and trying to test my psychic abilities?'

'The latter. Sorry about that.'

'Oh, it's quite all right. As long as I know what I'm up against, I can cope! Now,' she spread her fingers in the air and bent them over one at a time as she dealt with his questions, 'no, thank you, I won't have another brandy. Yes, that house was chaotic—the living room, at least. But that's only to be expected when you've got two young boys roaming around, bored because they've got colds. Yes, when you're viewing a house, you have to look beyond chaos, or horrid wallpaper, or whatever it is that they have and you wouldn't have. I adore children, and you are about to tell me now that you have two of them in quarantine, as well as your dogs, right?'

'Wrong!' Anton paused, serious now. 'How come you've never asked me whether I'm married?'

That train of thought was easy enough to follow. 'Because it would hardly affect me one way or the other.'

'Is that your stock answer?' He looked heavenward. 'I despair of you, Lorna. Couldn't you at least feign an interest?'

'All right,' she laughed. 'But I won't bother to ask the question. You've got bachelor written all over you.'

'Good grief! Am I so easy to read?'

She nodded and gave him an enigmatic smile. Actually, he asn't weasy to read. All she really knew about him was that he was a very persuasive man, with a great deal of charm. He made her laugh, he made her feel like an interesting person. His manner was relaxed, easy, and he had a way of drawing her into conversation without her even realising he was doing it. Was he, after all, a womaniser? Or was that her inbuilt cynicism coming into play? She couldn't help being cynical; it was part of her nature. He had not put a foot wrong, but she sure as hell didn't believe it was only friendship he was after. And even if it were, he was wasting his time.

Whether it was attributable this time to her train of thought, Lorna didn't know, but when Anton helped her into her coat, that awful feeling enveloped her again. It was the first time it had happened that day. It happened as she turned to face him when he had slipped her coat on to her shoulders. She felt her cheeks growing warm as she looked up at him, so tall, so powerful and attractive.

She looked away, feeling panicky, silly and suddenly warm. 'I—I've left my gloves on the chair.'

'I'll get them.'

The moment passed quickly, helped by the fact that Anton didn't seem to notice her blush, her sudden discomfiture. Within minutes she was at ease again—to the extent that she fell asleep in the car on the way back to The Lions!

Anton brought the car gently to a halt at the back of the house. He was loath to wake her, she looked so peaceful—peaceful and very beautiful. He kept his hands on the steering wheel, resisting the temptation to let his fingers trail over the smooth skin of her cheek, fighting the urge to take her in his arms. It wasn't easy, but he knew Lorna would not appreciate what he had in mind right now.

What he didn't know was why that was so.

Why, when the physical attraction was so strong between them, did she panic when he got too close to her? Panic was not too strong a word. He had seen it in her eyes just now in the bar, and not for the first time. But why, *why* was she afraid of him?

'That's super, Lorna! Thank you so much!' Eve surveyed herself in the full-length mirror in her bedroom. 'Shall I put some hairspray on?'

'You'd better. Just a touch.' Lorna nodded in satisfaction. She'd spent the past hour doing Eve's hair and the result was really effective. 'Put the dress on, then, so I can see the complete picture.'

She helped her friend into the carefully chosen red dress and laughed as Eve took hold of her hand and shook it vigorously. 'I take my hat off to you, Lorna. I look like a million dollars!'

'Your modesty is overwhelming. That was for me to say! Off you go, then. Your guests should start arriving any minute.'

Lorna went back to her own room. She hadn't even started getting ready for the party, apart from having bathed earlier. She took her time with her hair and make-up, then looked dubiously at the black dress she had laid on the bed. It was chiffon, cocktail-length and simplicity itself. It was perfect for tonight's affair. The trouble was that it was a little too revealing. It had very thin shoulder staps, a low neckline—if that's what one could call it—and she would be wearing it without a bra.

She slipped it on and examined herself critically in the mirror. She had had no doubts that the dress would be right; she still hadn't. It looked good, she looked good. But she was wondering what sort of effect the dress would have on Anton . . .

Cassandra was the first person Lorna spoke to when she went downstairs. She had brought her boy-friend with her, which was perhaps the reason why she seemed more confident than ever. He was dark and classically handsome and he couldn't take his eyes off Cassandra. Granted, Cassie looked gorgeous. The pale blue of her dress did wonders for her eyes and was the perfect foil for her black hair. The introduction to Cassie's boy-friend and the girls' exchange was brief, made only for appearances' sake. Lorna moved on into the drawing room, amused now by Cassie's hostility. The girl was a poor loser.

There were people everywhere, beautifully dressed and chatting away, creating an atmosphere quite unlike anything Lorna had known before. The drawing room had been cleared of much of its furniture, including the grand piano, which had been moved into the vast hall. A band had been brought in for the occasion and the music, for the moment at least, was quiet and unimposing. No doubt things would hot up a little when the party was fully under way.

Lorna was fascinated by it all. This party did have a novelty value for her. She chatted with people she had met on Christmas and Boxing Night, was introduced to umpteen new people, including Julian's parents, and was generally enjoying herself far more than she had expected to. On top of everything else there was still the feeling of Christmas in the air, the magnificent tree with its coloured lights lending a magical touch to the room.

She was sitting with Mrs Collingham when Anton walked in. 'I believe I'm tipsy,' the old lady was saying.

'Why, how many have you had?'

'Three—four, I think. What do you think?'

'What do I think? I haven't been counting!'

'No!' The old lady patted her hand. 'I didn't mean that! I meant—Ah, there's Anton. I say, doesn't he look splendid?' She beckoned to him as Lorna turned to look.

It was an understatement. Like most of the other men, he was wearing formal evening dress, but Anton had that certain ... what was it that made him stand out in a crowd? His height? That air of total confidence? His incredibly attractive smile?

Whatever, Lorna couldn't take her eyes from him. He was cutting a path towards her and she couldn't take her eyes from his. It was he who broke contact first by letting his eyes move slowly, approvingly, over the entire length of her. 'Stunning,' he said as he raised her hand to his lips. Lorna was so used to this gesture by now that she would have been disappointed had it not been forthcoming.

'Mary, you look charming. How are you this evening?'

Mrs Collingham beamed at him, telling him what she'd just told Lorna. 'And what do you think of my behaviour, Anton?'

'I think it's disgraceful.' He frowned, but he couldn't keep the laughter from his eyes. 'What are we going to do about her, Lorna? What will she be like when Michael makes his speech and the champagne starts flowing?'

'I dread to think.' Lorna was equally serious and Mrs Collingham laughed delightedly. 'I don't know about helping you to your room, I might have to carry you there if things continue like this! Or rather, Anton might.'

'But you haven't got a drink, Lorna,' Anton observed. 'Can I get you something?'

She told him what she would like and when he left her side, her eyes trailed after him.

'An exceptional man, isn't he?' Mrs Collingham said quietly.

'Yes,' Lorna answered without thinking. 'Yes, he is.' She frowned, still keeping him in sight. 'He ... he doesn't seem to take anything very seriously ...'

'Don't you believe it.' The tone of the old lady's voice was such that Lorna turned to face her. 'It's a case of the iron hand in a velvet glove, my dear. Ask Michael about him if you want to know more. Anton is a very determined man in his own quiet way. Michael thinks the world of him, you know.'

'Yes, so I've gathered.' Lorna shrugged. 'But I don't want to know more.'

'Of course you do.' Mrs Collingham smiled knowingly. 'And he's very taken with you, too. Can't say I blame him!'

Lorna couldn't help laughing. 'And you're not as tipsy as you make out, are you?'

'Keep it to yourself!' Mrs Collingham chuckled. 'I need to have some excuse for going to bed at eleven!'

That was just what she did. Lady Summers saw her to her room as the party really went into full swing. Sir Michael had made his speech about the engagement of Julian and Eve, the champagne was flowing, people were dancing, and the night was still young.

Lorna was chatting to some friends of Eve when Anton came to her. They had both circulated throughout the evening, as had everyone else, but she had known this moment was inevitable. When he asked her to dance, she excused herself from her company and accepted.

'I've waited a long time for this,' he murmured as his arm came around her. 'Dammit, my timing could have been better!'

As far as Lorna was concerned, his timing was perfect. The music had changed, and Anton was not pleased about it. The band were doing a splendid job of catering to a crowd comprising people of all ages. So they danced separately, in keeping with the music, and when it changed again some fifteen minutes later, Lorna excused herself.

'You're running out on me?' Anton protested.

'Yes.'

'You can't dance to slow music? Too young to know the proper way to dance, eh?'

'No.'

'Then you're avoiding me.'

'Yes.' She moved on to the sidelines, took a glass of champagne from one of the maids who were circulating and forced herself to keep a straight face. Anton was by her side, looking but saying nothing.

'I know you're not backward in coming forward, Anton,' Roger Summers' voice broke the silence, 'but if you're not interested in smooching with Lorna, I certainly am! Will you do me the honour, lovely lady?'

Lorna looked from Roger to Anton, placed her glass in the older man's hand and allowed Roger to lead her away. The idea of 'smooching' with Roger did not appeal to her in the least, but the thought of doing it with Anton appealed to her less. It was curious, though, the way she couldn't stop watching Anton while she danced with Roger, curious that the young man's arms around her provoked not the slightest reaction in her— panic, pleasure or anything else.

'I give up!' Roger let go of her after their first dance. 'My sister might not know when she's beaten, but I do.' He followed Lorna's eyes, smiling goodnaturedly. 'What's Anton got that I haven't?'

'I shouldn't be too sure about your sister.' Lorna was given a taste of her own medicine as she watched Cassie take Anton's arm and they joined the dancers.

So Lorna danced on with Roger until Julian intervened. She hit it off well with Julian, he was very easy to follow and a good dancer. The evening wore on and for a while she lost sight of Anton. Cassie had obviously taken him off somewhere. To meet her boy-friend, perhaps? To show Anton he wasn't the only attractive man around?

It was turned one o'clock and Lorna was dancing with Sir Michael when Anton reappeared. He tapped the older man on the shoulder. 'I believe this is my dance, Michael.'

'You want to dance with me? Anton, I didn't know you cared!'

Lorna giggled uncontrollably. She was not a drinker and the champagne had gone to her head.

'Michael, take your hands off that woman. Lorna and I agreed earlier we would have every dance after one o'clock.'

Sir Michael looked quite disappointed. 'Is this true, Lorna?'

'Absolutely not!'

'Then go away, Anton. Can't you see when you're not wanted? I haven't had such a good time for ages! Lorna dances my way, and I like that!'

Anton cleared his throat and whispered something in the older man's ear.

Sir Michael let go of her at once. 'Please excuse me.'

She found herself in Anton's arms before she had a chance to move. 'You rogue! What did you say to Sir Michael?'

He shrugged innocently. 'I told him his wife was looking for him.'

'And is she?'

'Of course not.'

Lorna relaxed as he led her, enjoying herself enormously and wondering what she had been worried about. He was lovely to dance with! Still, she was pretending annoyance. 'Have you no scruples?'

'Very few,' he murmured, pulling her just a little closer, 'when it comes to getting what I want.'

She looked up at him, a challenging look if ever there was one. 'And would you care to tell me exactly what it is you want?'

The broad shoulders shrugged slightly. 'Nothing sinister, green eyes, so take that suspicious look off your face. I want you to spend New Year's Day with me and show me around Windsor.'

'But——'

'Ah, ah—no excuses! *Feline* will be closed New Year's Day and I know you're leaving here that morning. I checked with Eve.'

'But you don't need me to give you a guided tour! And surely you've been to Windsor in the past?'

'Never.' He was lying in his teeth, but he forgave himself for it. 'I've never even seen the Castle, except for a glimpse from the motorway. I'm sure I'd find it interesting. As an architect, I mean.'

'I'm sure you would.' She knew he would. Lorna was proud of Windsor and felt sure Anton would like the place as much as she did. 'But the answer's no. I'll have work to do on New Year's Day.'

'Rubbish!'

'The answer's still no.'

'Look,' he said reasonably, appearing quite hurt, 'please don't say no—say maybe.'

'That sounds like an old song.'

'Don't change the subject.' He shook her slightly.

'All right, all right!' Dear lord, the man just wouldn't take no for an answer. So she agreed on maybe.

It was with a great deal of laughter that they found themselves dancing to that old song only five minutes later.

'I don't believe it!' Lorna was giggling like a schoolgirl. 'If I didn't know better, I'd swear you asked the band to play this!'

'Do you know better?'

'What? . . . Oh, Anton, you *didn't*!' But she wasn't sure. 'You couldn't have engineered our conversation to make it all fit! You couldn't have anticipated my answer about New Year's Day!'

'Couldn't I?' He said no more. He left it at that and closed the space between their bodies.

Lorna leaned her head against his shoulder, feeling happy and perfectly relaxed despite this physical closeness. But it didn't last, and when that dreadful feeling started to creep over her, she stiffened, unable to look at him. She was in danger of making a fool of herself.

'Relax, darling.' Anton's lips were close to her ear. She could feel the warmth of his breath on her cheek, the steady beat of his heart. She wanted to run away from him but could do no more than pull away slightly.

Her own heartbeat sounded loud in her ears, but the sense of panic was mingled with something else and it was seconds before she realised what it was. Unaccountable tears prickled at the back of her eyes as the realisation struck her, and she knew then that she had to get away from him, and fast. 'Please ...' she whispered, 'Anton, let go of me, please. I—it's so hot in here. I must get some air.'

He released her at once, but his hands caught hold of her elbows as she placed her palms against her cheeks. 'Lorna, what is it?'

'Nothing, I just——' Then their eyes met. She read concern in the brown depths of his eyes and saw the expression change as they moved over her face, resting briefly at the pulse which was throbbing at the base of her neck and then, fleetingly, his glance touched her breasts.

'Come.' He led her from the centre of the room and it took everything Lorna had not to run, to force herself to walk with some semblance of calmness and dignity.

She let go of his hand, turning, and managing, somehow, to smile. 'Thank you, I'm okay now. Goodnight.'

'Lorna——'

'Please! *Please* don't follow me. Goodnight, Anton.'

He let her go, cursing audibly in frustration, torn between chasing after her and doing as she'd asked. Added to that, he was baffled by her behaviour. He had seen for himself how she was feeling; what he didn't understand was why this upset her. Was she genuinely afraid of something ... or was she a master when it came to the art of teasing? 'The latter,' he muttered tersely. She'd been provoking him all evening, hadn't she? To hell with that, he thought as he went after her.

But Lorna was not in her room. She had known he would follow her and she'd headed for Eve's room on the other side of the house. Tears started streaming down her face before she even got there. She went into Eve's bathroom and splashed cold water on her face, but it didn't help. It didn't make her feel any less pathetic, less stupid.

Only tonight had she realised what it was she felt for Anton. She was not afraid of him. She *wanted* him! She was twenty-five years old and she had never, ever, experienced this before. No wonder she had been so slow to recognise it! All these years she had been convinced the man didn't exist who could have this effect on her. She wanted him physically, and *that* was what caused her to panic.

She was dizzy with confusion. At some level of her mind she was pleased to learn she was not abnormal, after all. Pleased that the terror of her experience with Jake had not driven her inside herself irredeemably. But the rest of her mind rejected Anton, the attraction he held for her and everything else about him. The fixed pattern in which she had been thinking for so many years could not easily be changed. Besides, she didn't want to change it.

She stayed where she was for a while, struggling with her emotions, her thoughts, confused and at a loss to understand what was happening to her, until she realised what she had to do. She must leave The Lions tomorrow. She must get away from the danger that was Anton and go home to the safety of her own world.

Finding him waiting in her bedroom didn't really surprise her. It irritated and embarrassed her.

'Sorry about the smoke in here. I've been waiting rather a long time.' He crushed out the cigarette he was smoking and hooked a leg over the arm of the chair he was in. His tie and the neck of his shirt were undone, his jacket was on the bed and he was infuriatingly relaxed.

'Please get out of here.' Lorna was by the door, holding it open.

'Close the door and sit down.'

'Anton——'

'Do it!'

It was the calm determination in his voice that made her do as he said. She thought of Mrs Collingham's comments about Anton, things she had known all the time, really. Beyond the charm, the good sense of humour, was a man with a strong personality and an equally strong will. She had long since realised this about him and, very reluctantly, she respected it.

She sat on the edge of the bed, well away from him, glad that there was only a single lamp burning so her face would be shadowed. 'All right, say your piece and then leave.'

'I'll leave when I'm ready. Come here.' He motioned her to the other armchair, and again there was something in his voice which brooked no argument.

She saw his expression change as she moved to the chair. 'Satisfied?'

'You've been crying.'

Lorna looked away, feeling ridiculous.

'You've been crying and I've been thinking. Hard. Now I'll have to think again—unless you're prepared to tell me what the hell you're afraid of. Is it me?'

'No,' she said simply, honestly. 'I just want you to get out of my life and stay out. I don't want involvement of any kind. I've told you several times, but you don't seem to believe me. I mean it, Anton. In my experience, when there are men in one's life, there's trouble. So just leave me alone. I can't be any plainer than that.'

There was a long silence before he answered. 'Lorna, you've been playing games with me and I haven't minded in the least—until an hour ago. I enjoy the fun of the chase just as much as the next man——'

'I don't know what you mean.' She looked at him properly for the first time. 'I'm not playing games with you.'

'But you are. Unwittingly, perhaps.' There was no laughter in his eyes, no jokes, no charm. There was just ... concern? 'You are as aware as I am of the attraction between us. It started the first time we saw each other, in Karel's house. Beyond all that was happening, your anger, your indignation, *it was there*. Now, are you going to deny it?'

'Yes.'

'After what happened to you when we were dancing?'

Lorna could feel herself going hot, her cheeks flaming. No, she couldn't deny it now, when only an hour ago her body had given him his answer. She couldn't speak.

'Okay,' he said quietly. 'We're making progress. I want you, Lorna. I came in here tonight with every intention of taking you to bed. I thought the occurrence when we were dancing signalled the end of the game—phase one, at least—that the affair which will inevitably take place between us was about to start. I'm sorry if this sounds cold-blooded or cynical, but I'm not naïve as far as women are concerned——'

She swore at him, all embarrassment forgotten. 'Cynical? It sounds bloody audacious! God, you're cool! Smooth, more like,' she added in disgust. 'Get out of here! Don't talk to me about inevitability! Who the hell do you think you are?'

Completely unperturbed by her outburst, he said, 'I'm being *honest* with you. Can't you respect that? I've told you how I feel.'

'Honest!' she scoffed. 'Two days ago you were offering friendship and nothing else!'

'I meant it. I still want your friendship. I like you very much, don't you realise that? And that's quite apart from what you do to me physically. So we'll keep sex out of it now, eh? You can call the tune as far as that's concerned, I give you my word on that. Now, I've said exactly what's on my mind, I've been absolutely honest with you. So will you tell me what it is you're afraid of?'

Dumbfounded, Lorna just looked at him. It was as if she were speaking to someone other than the Anton she knew. This was a different side to him. Yes, he was being honest. How could she be angry with him for that? But this—all of it—was so new to her, so completely beyond her experience, she was fazed.

'Please, Lorna, come on! Why the tears? Why did you run away and hide? Why are you scared by this attraction between us?'

When he was met with a long silence, Anton drew his own conclusions. 'You've had an affair that turned sour on you, is that it? It's something that happened quite recently and you're still hurting?'

She didn't know whether to laugh or cry. She did neither. His sincerity, that openness so characteristic of his expression, kept her eyes on his. She was quite mesmerised. Never had she met anyone remotely like him. And she wished she had never met him.

'You were in love—or you *are* in love with someone?' Anton was still probing, and still getting no answer. 'You've been hurt. It's obvious, Lorna! Why not tell me about it? It might help.'

Lorna was filled with an unaccountable sadness. She shook her head slightly, aware that tears were threatening again. 'I—perhaps—one day I might tell you.' She didn't mean it, she was saying it just to get rid of him. After tonight she had no intention of seeing him again—ever. 'Please—please go now. Go back to the party.'

He took hold of her hand and pulled her to her feet. 'I'm in no mood for that,' he said quietly. 'I'm going to my room.' Very gently he took her face between his hands, his fingers brushing lightly across her cheeks. 'Don't. No more tears. You'll tell me all about it, I know—in your own time, darling. There's no hurry . . . God, you're so beautiful . . .' He let go of her and reached for his jacket.

Lorna blinked back her tears as he turned to go. 'Anton——'

'Yes?'

'Please kiss me.'

He frowned, 'Lorna, I don't——'

'No,' she whispered, 'this isn't a game, either. Just . . . just kiss me. Please!'

He didn't embrace her, he just brushed her lips lightly with his own. He didn't pretend to understand this girl—not completely. But he had given her his word and he would not go back on it. She could call the tune.

Lorna knew this was wrong of her, that he would think her a tease, that she might be playing with fire and inviting trouble. But, while that was the last thing she wanted to do, she could not help herself. Once, just once, she wanted to know what it was like to be kissed by Anton. Her reasons were wholly selfish; she wanted to know how she would feel. It was an experiment, no more, no less.

The feeling of his lips brushing lightly against hers was pleasant in the extreme and brought in its immediate wake a feeling of confidence. She moved closer to him, placing her hands on his broad chest without breaking the contact of their lips. In those few seconds she was aware of so many things, so many sensations. Her hands were trembling slightly and, beneath them, she could feel Anton's heartbeat quickening.

She was aware of the clean, masculine smell of him; a faint whiff of aftershave and the clean-linen smell of his shirt. When his hands moved lightly over her back she was not alarmed, even though the power, the sheer strength of his body made her acutely aware of her vulnerability. Somehow she knew she was not in danger, she knew he was as much in control as she was. She opened her lips slightly, tasting the warm firmness of his own, feeling them part against her mouth as a barely audible groan escaped from them. His hands moved down her back, spanning the slenderness of her waist as he pulled her body closer to his and his kiss deepened.

She pulled away from him at once, her eyes searching his face. 'I ... don't be angry, Anton. I'm sorry.'

He couldn't hide his confusion. He shrugged, his smile fleeting and humourless. 'I'm not angry, my lovely. Not in the least.' Suddenly the humour was back. 'I'll tell you something, I've never been given such a chaste kiss. Not since I was twelve, at any rate.' He hooked his jacket over his shoulder, laughing now in spite of himself. 'And I'll tell you something else: I'll never forget it. Goodnight, Lorna.'

And then he was gone.

She stared after him as he gently closed the door, her fingers reaching up to brush her lips. But the spell had been broken when he left and sanity quickly returned. She went into the bathroom and patched up her make-up before going downstairs to find Eve. She had to tell her friend she was leaving first thing in the morning—though what excuse she would give, she had not yet worked out.

CHAPTER SEVEN

THE flat, the shop, were exactly as she had left them. Of course nothing had changed. In the middle of the afternoon Lorna went downstairs and just stood, looking around. The notice on the door said *Feline* would be open tomorrow, New Year's Eve, but not today. She wished she were open today; it would give her something to do. She had, in fact, nothing to do. Her books were up to date, she knew what she needed to buy in London next week, she knew what stock she was going to reduce for her forthcoming sale.

She switched on the lights, looking round almost cautiously as if she expected to find something missing, something wrong. The shop didn't feel the—the *same*, somehow. But then neither did her flat. She shook herself mentally as inspiration came. She would have a good clean up.

In an old pair of denims and a sweater, she set about it. There was little to do in the shop because it was kept immaculate always, so she concentrated on her flat and did the lot—kitchen floor, cooker, all the windows. Everything.

It helped only slightly, and when she settled down with a pot of tea in the middle of the evening, she scoffed at herself because only then did it dawn on her that her cleaning had been symbolic. The flat and the shop were just as they always had been. It was *she* who was different. She felt different . . . as if she had come back from Hampshire with a new dimension to her personality. And she wanted to get rid of it.

But she could not get rid of it by cleaning. If it really existed at all. If it did, she could only think her way out of it, exorcise it with rational thinking. Of one thing she was certain: the inner peace she valued so much had

113

been disturbed well and truly. By Anton. How very typical that a man was the root cause of this—again. But not for long! She would dismiss him, *this minute*, from her thoughts.

She had had no choice but to come clean with Eve. At least, when she had asked Lorna whether she had had a row with Anton, Lorna said yes, sort of.

'Sort of?' She and Eve had gone into Sir Michael's study, which was the only downstairs room where they could be sure of some privacy. 'What does that mean, Lorna?'

'It means he's altogether too ... too ...'

'Keen?'

'Yes. Look, Eve, I'm really not interested. I want to avoid him, if the truth's known.'

Eve frowned, doing her best not to pry but unable to help herself. 'I'm stumped. I know you like him—you can't deny it. Personally, I think he's gorgeous. Oh, I'm not just talking about his looks. I mean, he's got everything!'

'Then let's call it a personality clash. I want to go before breakfast, Eve. I don't want to have to see him again, okay? My only concern is that your parents don't misunderstand why I'm leaving——'

'Oh, don't worry about that!' Eve laughed. 'I'll simply tell them the truth. So what? They'll understand.'

'No! Tell them, and tell Anton—er—you could say I had an early phone call from Dulcie saying she's got 'flu. Tell them I had to go home to get things ready for opening New Year's Eve. Will you do that?'

'I'll dream up a good excuse.' Eve shrugged, amused by it all. 'But I warn you now—Anton will come after you.'

'He won't. I've made it very clear to him I'm not interested.'

Eve opened her mouth to speak, but thought better of it. 'You're crazy,' she said at length. 'But you win. I'll give him and my parents a convincing story.'

Lorna washed up her teacup, decided against having something to eat, took a hot bath and went to bed. But Anton Van der Buren was still on her mind at three o'clock in the morning.

Dulcie arrived at the shop at five to ten the next day, as punctual as ever. 'Lorna! What on earth are you doing here? I thought—You don't look yourself. Are you unwell?' Before Lorna had a chance to answer she went on, smiling. 'Too much of the high life, eh? Too much to eat, too much to drink, and you're feeling liverish. Is that it?'

'Something like that. I'd had enough, Dulcie. Oh, it was all very nice, but I'd had enough. Come on, the kettle's on.'

Inevitably, Dulcie asked about her stay at The Lions, and Lorna told her as much as she wanted her to know. She mentioned Anton, but only in passing, giving no more importance to his presence than she did to anyone else's. She couldn't not mention him, not when Eve would be bound to do so at some future point.

As soon as she could, she switched the topic to Dulcie and asked what had happened to her over Christmas. By eleven-thirty they were still sitting in the stockroom, chatting, and not one customer had crossed the threshold.

'It looks as if opening was a complete waste of time. I'm sorry, Dulcie. Feel free to go home, won't you?'

'Thanks, but I'll stay. Till four, at least. To tell you the truth, I'm glad to be back at work. All my visitors left last night and my husband's taking me to a dinner dance tonight, so I've got nothing to do at home.' She laughed. 'Let's put it this way: there's nothing I want to do at home. The cleaning up can wait until I've got my daily to help me.'

'You get bored if you spend too much time in the house, don't you?'

'Yes. I—I suppose it would have been different if we'd been able to have children.'

By three o'clock there had been several customers

and enough sales to warrant opening, though they were not rushed off their feet. They took it in turns to see to the customers, and much to her annoyance, Lorna's mind kept going back to Anton immediately she had nothing to distract her. Added to that she was irritated because Dulcie was not convinced by Lorna's paltry excuse for returning to work. She didn't ask more questions, she knew better than to do that, but her curiosity was unmistakable.

Early in the evening Lorna made herself a snack and put the radio on. She hadn't known such discontentment in a long, long time. She read again the postcard which had come from Cathy, read the advert which had been enclosed with her telephone bill and glanced at the statements which were due to be paid this month. She tried to settle down to a new novel she had recently bought, but even that didn't hold her attention. The television was her last resort, and it worked. She was deeply engrossed in a film when the doorbell brought her to her feet, and her first reaction was one of resentment at the intrusion. The film was about to end in ten minutes, and it was a real cliff-hanger.

'Damn!' She got up, then stood stock still, knowing who was at the door. 'Oh, dammit, no!' How was she going to rid him from her mind if he kept turning up in her life—like a bad penny?

'Anton, don't lean against the door!' she yelled at him through the glass. 'You'll trip the burglar alarm—it's on a trembler system.' She fiddled with the locks, trying not to smile as he waved a bottle of champagne at her. The man was incorrigible!

'I say,' he stepped inside as she opened the door, 'this is very, very smart. Super.' He nodded approvingly as he glanced round the shop.

'Thank you. Now, what do you want?'

'What a welcome! I came to wish you a Happy New Year.'

'It's only nine o'clock, you're a bit premature.'

'Well,' he grinned, 'I had to allow time for this to

chill.' He thrust the champagne at her. 'Lead the way, my lovely.'

She shook her head, not knowing what she was going to do about him. 'Why aren't you at Sir Michael's party?'

'Because I'm having my own party tonight.' He kissed her on the nose and she waved him away impatiently. 'They know I want to spend what's left of my time with you. They not only understood but approved. You made a very good impression on them, you know.'

'I'm not out to impress anyone,' Lorna said stubbornly, 'you, especially.'

'Ah, but you have! Take me to your boudoir.'

She led the way upstairs, suppressing her laughter with difficulty. As they got into her living room she turned to find him looking around with interest, the brown eyes serious now.

'This is charming, Lorna. You've managed to make it very . . . cottage-like. And who sent you these flowers, I wonder?'

'I bought them myself,' she shrugged. 'I like fresh flowers in a room. At this time of year they're an indulgence, but I enjoy them.'

'And this?' He went to take a closer look at a framed photograph on a wall, one that Lorna had had enlarged. It was a very simple but beautiful photo of an old stone wall with a weeping willow in the foreground. 'I like this—very much. Who took it?'

'I did.' She was pleased. 'I love the colours in the old wall, the tree, the—Oh, I don't know—the general . . .'

'Balance,' he provided. 'You're interested in photography, then?'

'No, it was just a fluke. I'll show you the original snap, if you like.'

'Yes. And may I see the rest of the flat?'

'All right,' she smiled. 'Give me your coat. I'll just put this bottle in the fridge.'

Anton followed her into the kitchen and she showed

him what little there was to see of the rest of the flat. 'It
isn't finished yet.' She told him about the other things
she wanted to buy for the living room, the tables and
lamps and so on. 'I should be able to afford them this
year.' She looked up to find him watching her, his
expression unreadable.

'The place has a nice feeling about it. It helps me to
know you better.'

'It does?'

'And that wooden carving over there—did you buy it
or was it a gift? It's beautiful.'

'I think so.' Lorna picked it up, letting her fingers
trail over the smooth planes of the wood. 'It was very
expensive.' She laughed delightedly, her eyes sparkling
with mischief. 'It cost twenty-five shillings!'

'You're joking.'

'No. That'll tell you how long ago it was. I found it
in a junk shop when I was a teenager.'

It was only when Lorna found herself cooking
chicken and chips half an hour later that she realised
how she had once again given in to Anton. She hadn't
even intended to let him into her flat! But here he was,
and when he'd asked her whether she would like to go
out to eat, she'd offered to cook! She could hardly
credit what was happening, could hardly believe her
own behaviour.

At midnight they went outside to bring the New Year
in, hurried back to the warmth of the flat and opened
the champagne.

'To the year ahead.' Anton raised his glass in a toast.
'I wanted to be with you tonight—now—so we might
bring in the New Year together.'

Lorna just nodded and drank, not quite knowing
what to say. They were standing by the fire. Anton put
his glass down and cupped her face in his hands. 'A kiss
for New Year, Lorna? Do you mind?'

Wordlessly she shook her head and he kissed her
briefly, lightly, his eyes crinkling with amusement as he
raised his head. 'Chaste kiss number two.'

He left shortly after that. She watched him stifling a yawn as he got up from the settee, stretching lazily, his arms almost touching the ceiling as he did so. 'Are you driving back to Hampshire, Anton?'

'No, no. I've booked into a hotel in the High Street here—the Castle.'

'I know it well. Eve and I often pop into their coffee shop.'

'Eve recommended it,' he grinned. 'I must go. We'll want to make a reasonably early start in the morning.'

'What?' She had no idea what he meant.

'You're giving me a guided tour, remember? How does ten o'clock suit you.'

'But—but I only said maybe!'

'Would nine be better?'

'Anton, I've met some cheeky people in my time, but you take the biscuit!'

'I don't know what you mean,' he said innocently. 'I'm afraid my English isn't that good.'

Lorna's mouth fell open. 'I've heard everything now!' But she had the feeling she'd end up agreeing to this date, and after a few minutes of Anton's gentle persuasion, she did just that. 'All right. Ten o'clock will be fine.'

It was a glorious day. It was cold and crisp, but there wasn't a cloud in the sky. Lorna showed Anton everything there was to see, by car and on foot. A lot of places were closed, of course, being out of season and New Year's Day to boot, but their day was crammed with activity. They had lunch in Old Windsor, then drove around the surrounding country-side for an hour.

It was seven o'clock when they got back to *Feline* and Anton said he would call back for her at eight-thirty, that they would have dinner in his hotel. She bathed, put on fresh make-up and slipped into a smart but simple knitted dress.

They had a drink in the hotel's bar first, and it was only then that she realised he was going back to

Holland the next day. She honestly could not tell whether she was relieved or disappointed.

'I—didn't realise you were going back so soon.'

'For a couple of weeks,' he said. 'I'll have to make several trips back and forth before I finally settle here ... when I finally settle. The house business is proving quite a problem. But I'll use a hotel as a base until I find something suitable.'

'Won't you stay with Karel?'

'Heavens, no. Oh, I do stay there occasionally, but only if he's away! At least, we only overlap by a couple of days.'

'Sounds an odd sort of arrangement. Don't you get on with your cousin?'

'Yes,' he smiled. 'But only in short doses. Basically we have nothing in common, but he's a nice enough chap. A bit zany.'

Lorna looked at him suspiciously. 'What you really mean is you would cramp his style if you stayed with him any length of time. You could hardly play gooseberry on the evenings he's entertaining his girl-friends.'

'Lorna!' Anton put his hand on his heart. 'What do you think of the Van der Burens? You wound me!'

'That they're smooth operators,' she said bluntly. 'You and your cousin, at least.'

He shook his head at her. 'Come on, madam, let's go and eat.'

They moved into the elegant atmosphere of the restaurant with its gold and white décor, its immaculately clad waiters, and Lorna ate far more than she normally did. The day had given her an appetite.

At length she sat back, replete, content, not minding when Anton reached for her hand. 'That was lovely. Thank you.'

'Lorna, I'll come back to England as soon as I can. I'm not quite free of my business yet, but I'll be counting the days until I see you again.'

'No, Anton.' She pulled her hand from his. 'I want this to be goodbye. It's been nice meeting you and I've

enjoyed today very much. But this is it. Basically, you
and I have nothing in common——'

'What nonsense! How can you say that?'

'Well,' she hedged, 'it's just ... Look, I don't *want*
any involvement. I've told you repeatedly——'

'But you're already involved.'

'What do you mean?'

'Aren't you?'

Was she? Dammit, *was* she? She lowered her eyes
from his scrutiny, unable to think straight when she was
looking directly into those eyes of his. She didn't want
to see his smile, those ruggedly attractive features, the
strong lines of his face which told of his determination.
'No.' She made herself look at him then. 'No, I'm not.
There's only one thing I'm involved with and that's my
shop. It means everything to me, and I'm very, very
happy with my life just as it is.'

He considered this for a long moment. 'And content?'

'Yes. That too.'

'You worry me, Lorna.' He covered her hand with
his. 'You shouldn't build your life on only one support.
I'm speaking from experience. If you allow one single
element to become your support in life—such as
business—then God help you if something happens to
take that away from you. There should be other things
in life which also make you happy. There should be
some variety and——'

'Nothing will take *Feline* away from me,' she said
vehemently. 'Nothing.'

'I don't think you understand what I mean. Let me
put it another way——'

'No, I haven't misunderstood.' She looked at him
levelly. 'There is nothing else I want. I don't *want*
anything else in my life. Please take me home now. I'm
quite tired.'

He did as she asked, unhurriedly but without
argument. When they reached the door of her shop he
insisted on seeing her safely inside, but she put her foot
down when he invited himself to stay for coffee.

'No, Anton, I'm tired. Really.'

'Is that the only reason? Or is it that you still don't trust me?'

'Yes. No. I mean——' Of course she didn't trust him. Yet she couldn't bring herself to say it when he still hadn't even attempted to make a pass at her. 'I mean I'm tired, that's all. Goodbye, Anton. Bon voyage.'

'I'll see you soon, Lorna.'

'No.'

'Maybe?'

'*No.*'

He left, laughing at her, and she turned away in frustration as he waved at her through the shop window. He would be back. She had no doubt about it. What the devil was she going to do about him?

A few days later, when life had settled into some semblance of normality, Lorna drove into London to meet Cathy for lunch and to do some buying. The January sales were on and business was quite perky.

She let her sister do the talking first, telling her about her holiday in the Canary Islands, then watched Cathy's face as she listened with rapt attention to all that had happened to Lorna. As Lorna had predicted, Cathy took the news of her meeting with Anton with a great deal of hilarity, but by the time Lorna got to the end of the story the younger girl was as bewildered by it all as Lorna was.

'If I didn't know this was impossible, I'd swear you'd fallen in love with him!' Cathy shook her head, incredulous.

'Well, it is impossible, so don't talk so stupidly.'

'But Lorna! Lorna, you've never before given in like this. You never give an inch as far as men are concerned. And this man has taken a mile!'

'I know. I—but it's over now. It won't happen again.'

'But why, for heaven's sake? Why not, if you like him?'

Lorna glared at her. 'You, of all people, shouldn't need to ask me that.'

Cathy groaned unhappily. 'Oh, Lorna! You can't stay as you are for ever. You're only half alive. Don't let the past continue to haunt you. I know it's easy for me to say, but——'

'Yes, it is easy to say,' Lorna snapped. She had told her sister everything, every detail of her time with Anton. But Cathy could not really understand Lorna's fears. Oh, she knew all the facts about Jake Dougan, but she hadn't been on the receiving end of his attack. 'I'm ... I can't help the way I am, Cathy. You see, I just ... it's so hard to explain. There were moments with Anton when I was so panic-stricken I could hardly breathe. This—this feeling that comes over me, it—it's almost suffocating.'

Cathy's eyes were filled with concern. 'But as time passed it got better. Didn't it? You just said——'

'I know what I said.' Lorna looked around the restaurant and lowered her voice to a whisper. 'I did—want him—sort of. Yes, I was aroused, but—but I couldn't do anything about it. My fear is stronger than my desire, by a long way.'

'I'm trying to understand,' Cathy sighed. 'I *do* understand, but ... well, I think perhaps you should see a psychiatrist.'

Lorna was furious at the suggestion. 'I'm perfectly well aware of what happens in my own mind, Cathy! I don't need a shrink to tell me!'

'All right, all right, don't bite my head off! But why not tell Anton? Tell him. It'll help him to understand.'

'Because I'm ashamed of it, dammit! I'm ashamed!' Lorna spoke so loudly that people in the restaurant turned to look at her. She dropped her voice. 'Besides, he's only after one thing, just like the rest of them! And why should I force myself into doing something I don't even want to do?' she hissed. 'You might have affairs willy-nilly—so might he. But I don't. And won't!'

'And can't.' Cathy pulled no punches. 'You keep contradicting yourself. A minute ago you admitted you find him exciting. You said you were aroused but you couldn't do anything about it—which implies that you want to.'

'Shut up! Leave me alone.' Lorna put her hands to her temples, sighing. 'I'm sorry, Cathy. We're fighting again.'

'Yes. Well, if you're really not interested in having an affair with Anton, the problem will solve itself. He doesn't sound like the type who'd last long in a purely platonic relationship.'

'That suits me fine,' Lorna said airily. 'At least I can look on his return as only a temporary nuisance.'

'How long do you think you can go through life like this?' Cathy looked at her in despair. 'I'm not sure what's holding you back, Lorna, your very understandable hang-ups or your morals! Have an affair with him! Take life as it comes. I would, I'll tell you, and I'd get what I could from him while I was at it.'

Lorna was appalled—by all of this. 'What's that supposed to mean?'

Cathy leaned closer, talking to Lorna as if she were an innocent. 'More and more I'm coming to the conclusion that men are to be exploited. That's what I mean. They use women, why shouldn't we use them? Anton is very very rich. Karel told me that Anton's side of the family were industrialists, they were in steel for generations. Your would-be lover has inherited a bundle—quite apart from what he's made himself!'

'I'm not interested in that!' Lorna said it harshly, and she meant it. She looked at Cathy as if she had never seen her before. 'I don't know what's happening to you, Cathy. Whatever it is, I don't like it.'

'I thought we made a pact. Live and let live. One man's meat and all that.'

Lorna was quiet for a long time. She couldn't, wouldn't, talk to Cathy about Anton ever again. His words came floating back to her . . . 'You are not your brother's keeper.' She reminded herself of the truth in the saying and when next she spoke, she switched the subject to the advertisements Cathy was working on.

She got back to Windsor feeling more disturbed than ever—about Cathy, about Anton, about the confusion in her own mind. Cathy had been right about one thing—Lorna was full of contradictions just now, though she hated to admit it.

It was almost closing time when Eve came round to see her. Lorna saw her assistant out and then locked up and took Eve upstairs for a cup of tea.

'Sorry I haven't been round sooner. Isn't it miserable, being back at work?' Eve sank wearily into a chair.

'I've been back for days. And no, it's lovely. Did you have an extended holiday or something?'

'Lovely? That's typical of you! Yes, I've been with Julian, staying at his parents' place for a few days in Devon. We've set the wedding date—finally.'

'Really? That's great! When is it?'

'The last Saturday in April. I'll start looking for a dress soon.'

'I can't help you there, I'm afraid. For you, that will mean Harrods or somewhere like that.'

'Quite. Mummy will sort it out, no doubt. Now come on, enough of me! What about you and Anton?'

'There's nothing to tell. I'll put the kettle on.'

'Lorna!' Eve came close to a shriek. 'Forget tea. I can't stay, anyhow. Come on! Where did he take you on New Year's Eve? I'll bet it was very romantic. Where did he wine you and dine you?'

'Here,' Lorna said drily. 'We stayed in and had frozen chicken and frozen chips.'

'Frozen . . .? Now I've heard everything!' Eve was very let down.

'And champagne at midnight,' Lorna was biting her cheeks.

'We-ell, that's a slight improvement.' She brightened. 'And New Year's Day? Where did you go? I can't help it, Lorna, I want to know all!'

'Windsor,' Lorna was enjoying this. 'He asked me to show him our lovely town, so I gave him a guided tour.'

'*What?*' Eve sat up in her chair. 'I can't believe this. What did he do that for? Anton spent several years at Eton, must know Windsor better than you do!'

It was Lorna's turn to be dumbstruck. But she was not let down. The more she thought about it, the funnier it became. She ended up prostrate with laughter, visualising herself and Anton standing on the bridge which spans the Thames, which separates the town of Eton from Windsor. She'd been pointing out the cast-iron work of the bridge and then she had pointed to Eton High Street. 'Just along there is the famous school. You must have heard of it. Come on, I'll show it to you.' Then she had taken pains to point out the varied examples of domestic architecture which grace the High Street, telling him how it dated back to fourteen hundred and something.

'The rogue! The *rogue*,' she said to Eve. 'Isn't he the limit! There I was, telling him the bit that I know, and there he was, feigning fascination! Him and his gentle persuasion—him and his lies!'

'Gentle persuasion? Lorna, what *are* you talking about?' Eve didn't find this at all funny.

'Never mind.' Lorna was trying to stop laughing. 'Let's just say that so far I've been unable to insult him, to put him off, to anger him or to resist him. He just finds ways of getting round me, and this was one of them. He picked for a day's outing something I would especially enjoy!'

There was only one remark which made sense to Eve. 'Unable to resist him?'

Lorna looked heavenward. 'Now you're prying. The strength of his personality, that's all I meant!'

'Oh. Pity. I thought we might make it a double wedding.'

'Think again.' Lorna sobered completely. 'Oh, I know he'll be back, but it won't last.'

Anton stayed in Holland longer than expected and

during the three weeks he was away, Lorna went through various, and varied, phases. By the end of the first week she had talked about him and thought about him to such an extent that she was really angry with herself. In the early part of the second week she acknowledged that the impact Anton had had on her had hit her like the proverbial ton of bricks. And she had thought it would, could, never happen to her. Not to her.

In her most cynical moods she thought of him as clever, and she realised she had underestimated his cleverness, his shrewdness. He was a charmer, a manipulator and cunning with it. In her more reasonable, rational moments, she knew instinctively that he was sincere and honest, and the sort of friend she should be pleased to have . . .

Which led to the next thought.

. . . In her heart of hearts, where rationalisations, lies and excuses are inadmissible, she wanted him physically. If any man could make a full-blooded woman out of her, it was Anton Van der Buren. If only she could be just a little like Cathy—just a little. If only she could have an affair, take life as it comes. She wanted nothing from him except that which he would be only too pleased to give.

By the start of the third week, when Lorna had absorbed all that had gone through her mind, she rejected it. All of it. Perhaps it was because of his absence. She was settling into her old routine again, without his physical presence to influence her. He had telephoned her several times—as if he were determined she wouldn't forget him—but that was not the same as seeing him.

So it was that by the end of the third week, Lorna had everything perfectly in perspective. She, her thoughts and her emotions were no longer confused. She had reached a conclusion, a balanced, sensible conclusion. She would see Anton occasionally, she decided. Just occasionally. She did not want to cut him out of her life, nor would she get too involved. She would run her life exactly as she had been running it for the past year except that she would allow him to be her friend. That way, she would not invite trouble of *any* kind.

Anton phoned and told her he would be back in England on the Friday of the third week of January. Lorna agreed to have dinner with him. On the Thursday evening she was doing the shop window, as usual, which was something she really enjoyed, when she suddenly looked up and saw him standing in the street, watching her.

She was barefooted, clad in faded denims and an old sweater, wriggling around on the floor of the window-setting in the most ungainly manner. She shot to her feet as she spotted Anton, feeling happy and foolish, afraid and excited.

'Hello, Anton. You—you're a day early.' Her mouth was dry.

For once in his life Anton couldn't think what to say. He had never before seen her looking anything less than immaculate ... and he had never seen her looking as beautiful as she did now. Without her shoes she had to look up at him directly, and her eyes—her eyes—they were telling him she was glad to see him.

Had she missed him as much as he had missed her? Had she thought about him every day? Could he tell her now that he was in love with her? Was she ready for this? Could he tell her he never wanted to be parted from her again, that he had realised as soon as he left England that he had started to love her right from the beginning?

She was saying something about coffee, and he managed a flippant reply. No, this was no time for declarations. It was far, far too early for that. It took every ounce of his control not to reach for her ... but he had given her his word. For the first time in his life, he felt humble. He had not anticipated that he would fall deeply in love with her. He had never loved a woman the way he loved Lorna. He hadn't even been close to it.

Lorna's heartbeat accelerated as she climbed the stairs to the flat, but the stairs were not responsible for it. She hadn't anticipated this . . . this pleasure on seeing him again. The image of him was still in her mind, of the way he had looked when she saw him standing in the light from the streetlamp. The light was catching on his hair so that it looked like the colour of antique gold. He was smiling, as he did so easily, smiling in that special way he had.

'Let me take your coat——' She turned to face him. He had already discarded his overcoat and she saw he was dressed casually in a rollneck sweater and plain black slacks. Without another word she reached for him, slipping her arms around his neck and inviting his kiss.

She was conscious of and frustrated by his restraint. She pressed closer to him, letting instinct teach her things she should by now be well versed in. 'Anton . . .'

CHAPTER EIGHT

SHE spoke his name against his lips, heard his sharp intake of breath as his mouth claimed hers in an exquisitely sensuous kiss which set every nerve in her body tingling, sent the blood pounding through her veins. Her own restraint was non-existent, she responded fully, willingly, joyous in the feeling of his chest pressing against the softness of her breasts, conscious of the way they were responding so naturally to this contact.

And then his restraint was gone. 'Oh, God, Lorna——' His response was so ardent, so immediate! He pulled her closer so that every inch of her body was pressed tightly against him. His hands moved under her sweater and slid slowly, smoothly towards her breasts ... and with the movement came that suffocating fear. She stilled his hands at once, her breath catching in her throat as she saw the look in his eyes. Dear God, if he was angry with her ... Her heart was hammering against her ribs but passion had nothing to do with it now.

'Nothing has changed, then?'

She just looked at him. She couldn't believe he was smiling. He was angry with her; she knew full well he was angry with her.

'Lorna, don't—don't look at me like that! What is it?' He reached for her, alarmed, disturbed at what he saw in her face. 'Darling, what *is* it?'

'Don't!' She stepped away from him, her hands raised in an attitude of defence. 'Anton, I'm sorry. I won't— I'll never . . .'

'Lorna?'

'I—it's just—you look so—so tall tonight. So—so big.'

'What?'

She laughed nervously. 'I—never realised quite how

tall you are. Perhaps I should put some shoes on! But first I'll make your drink.'

'Crazy!' He ran his fingers through his hair. 'The girl is crazy.' He was laughing now. 'About me, of course.'

'Oh yes? Tea or coffee?'

'Have you got anything stronger? I could use a drink.'

'Only brandy, I'm afraid.'

'That'll do. Neat, please. Jump to it! Don't just stand there looking seductive. One of these days you'll get more than you've bargained for, young woman.'

Lorna escaped into the kitchen, his last sentence ringing in her ears. She would never, ever, behave like that again. Was she out of her mind or something?

They chatted for a while, mainly about what he'd been doing in Amsterdam, before they went out to dinner. She had already learned that he had a father and a stepmother at home in Holland, plus two brothers, both of whom were older than he and married. The rest of the Van der Burens, the less wealthy side of the family, were living in Kent, England, except for Karel.

'And what about your house in Amsterdam?' she asked. 'What are you going to do about that? Will you keep it on?'

'No. It's up for sale. Which reminds me, did you get those copies of *Country Life* for me?'

'Yes.' Lorna fetched them for him. 'Three weeks' issues. There are two houses in last week's and several in this week's which might interest you.'

'Good.' He flicked through the pages, looking firstly at the ones where Lorna had stuck a bit of paper between them. 'This one's of no interest, Lorna. Nor this.' He looked up, grinning. 'The first two I've looked at are in north Buckinghamshire—they're too far away! Are you trying to get rid of me or something?'

'Well . . .' This reminded her of her conversation with Eve. 'Your knowledge of England's geography is very good. And I'm told you know Windsor like the back of your hand . . .'

He could tell from her eyes she wasn't angry. His grin changed into a smile. 'Eve?'

'Eve. I'll go and change while you're looking at those.'

When she emerged from her bedroom he was looking decidedly pleased with himself. 'You're looking very lovely, Miss Stewart. Nice dress. But I've come to the conclusion you'd look good in anything.'

'Not the clothes I was wearing ten minutes ago.'

'Especially the clothes you were wearing ten minutes ago. Those jeans fit you like a second skin. I approved very much.'

'That was my off-duty image. There are different sides to me, you know.'

'Who are you telling? Look, come and see. I've found a house. It's perfect.'

He flicked the magazine open and Lorna suppressed a smile. It was the house she would have chosen had she been able to afford such an extravagance. It was gorgeous. It was also in Berkshire, not very far from Windsor . . . which was why she hadn't pointed it out to him. If he bought it, he would be a little too close for comfort . . .

'Vacant possession, too,' he muttered, eyeing the photograph thoughtfully.

'They don't quote a price . . . And it's old. It might be structurally unsound. Still, I suppose you will be your own surveyor.'

'Quite.' He was laughing at her rather than with her. 'And you would rather I went to live in Scotland.'

'My dear, I didn't say that! Australia would do just as well.'

'We'll view it tomorrow.' He dropped the magazine.

'We?'

'Come on. I'm hungry.'

She would stick to her resolve. She would stick to it no matter what and just see him occasionally. It was true that she felt closer to him, that it was as if they had not been separated for three weeks, but the man was under her skin, and it bothered her very much.

Anton called it a 'medium' sized house. It was actually an eighteenth-century stone-built farmhouse, and the interior had been cleverly, beautifully modernised. It had been extended some years earlier and with six bedrooms and three bathrooms, in Lorna's opinion it was big. At the back of the house, also built from stone, there was a small staff cottage. Adjacent to that there were paddocks and a stone barn and the properties stood in seven acres of ground.

She thought it was out of this world.

They spent a long time looking it over. If the agent who had met them there grew impatient or bored while Anton examined every inch of the place, the man didn't show it. Anton took his time, notebook and pen at the ready, and when he had seen all he wanted to see, Lorna went to wait in the car while the two men talked business.

'I've made an offer for it.' Anton joined her in the car but made no attempt to start it. 'The owners are asking too much and the agent knows it. However——'

'You're going to buy it? Just like that?'

'It's what I want,' he said simply. 'It has the right feel about it. Don't you see what I mean?'

She smiled. She hadn't meant that. She was thinking how nice it was for him that he could indulge like this. 'I know exactly what you mean. As the blurb in the magazine said—it's charming.'

'I shall convert the barn into a studio,' he informed her. 'And that's where I shall do my work.' He grinned, 'I shan't rush it, though—the conversion, I mean.'

'You mean you'll do it yourself? You, personally?'

'Why not? I'd enjoy that. As for the house itself, will you help me, Lorna? Help me to furnish, decorate and so on?'

'I'd love to! I can't decorate, though, I'm hopeless.'

'No, no, I'll get people in to do that. I mean will you

help me to choose things—everything? You can have carte blanche—do with it as you will.'

She was suddenly uneasy. She could have carte blanche? What was this supposed to mean? 'No. No, I won't help you.' She said it firmly.

'But you just said you'd love to——'

'No. I—It's—the answer's no. You must put your own stamp on the place. It must be you, you must put in your own feeling, as you call it.'

'Lorna . . .'

She was adamant, and for once his gentle persuasion didn't work. 'For once, Anton, you must take no for an answer.'

He started the car, his warm brown eyes quite villainous. 'May I remind you, madam, that I do know how to take no for an answer. Or have you forgotten that this won't be the first time?'

Lorna turned to look out of the window. There was no answer to that.

Anton dropped her at the shop in the middle of the afternoon, and Lorna had no choice but to tell Dulcie that he was making an offer for the house. He had worked his magic on Lorna's assistant when he had walked into the shop a few hours earlier. He had introduced himself because Lorna was busy with a customer. He had also told her of the 'unforgettable Christmas' he had shared with Lorna at The Lions. Of course Dulcie had given him every encouragement to chat, had let him know Lorna had mentioned him to her when telling her about her stay with Sir Michael Summers.

Then Anton had gone on to tell Dulcie he was taking Lorna out to lunch, then to view a house, so Dulcie's questions were inevitable now. 'How exciting! And will you help him to get settled in, Lorna?'

'Of course not. He's only an acquaintance, you know.'

'When will he move in?'

'As soon as possible, he says. He'll move in as soon

as he's got a bed in there, then do the place up at his leisure. I shouldn't think it'll take long. Eve will do the conveyancing. He's gone to see her now.'

'But in the meantime he's staying here in Windsor. Is Eve putting him up? Or her fiancé, perhaps?'

'No, he's staying in a hotel.'

'Really?' Dulcie's amusement was unmistakable. 'Which one?'

'The Castle.'

'So close, eh? You'll probably be seeing a lot more of him, then?'

Lorna didn't answer that one. She pretended not to hear.

'I thought him charming.' Dulcie was undeterred.

'Very,' Lorna said stiffly.

'And extremely attractive . . .'

Lorna didn't bother to deny it. 'Very.' She shrugged, saying the word as nonchalantly as she could.

Her one-word answers worked. Dulcie got the message and asked nothing further. For the moment, at least. But Lorna would, she knew, have to live with her assistant's curiosity from now on—and her obvious delight, not to mention surprise.

It was by no means easy, but Lorna did stick to her resolve, sort of, over the next few weeks. She met Anton for lunch occasionally and they saw each other two or three evenings a week. It was, in fact, more than she had intended to see of him, but it was still less frequent than it would have been had he had his way.

Fortunately for her, she had a will that was almost equal to his own. Almost. And yet . . . and yet on the nights when she was alone she felt lonely. She never used to feel like that. The flat used to be a sanctuary to her, a peaceful place where she never felt lonely or bored.

But now, when Anton wasn't with her she found herself thinking about him. He was so good to be with. They stayed in only a couple of times, during a week when Lorna had a bit of a cold, but apart from that they drove into London and went to see a show or they went out into the countryside to have dinner. He had stopped inviting himself in for coffee—and Lorna didn't encourage it.

Somewhere inside her she knew that something would have to give. Things could not go on for ever as they were. She thought several times of Cathy's remark—that Anton would not last long in a platonic relationship. Well, so far he had.

But for how much longer?

Towards the end of March he went back to Holland for five days. He urged Lorna to go with him, but she refused and stood firm on her decision. She used her business as a reason for not joining him even while the idea of going abroad, of seeing his native country, appealed to her very much. Knowing how important *Feline* was to her, Anton reluctantly stopped arguing.

It was when he came back from his trip that she told him her life story. He had moved into his house—into one room of it, at least—and Lorna hadn't seen the place since she viewed it with him. He wouldn't let her see it until it was finished. Whether he was doing this out of pique because she had refused to help him, she didn't know. Anyway, it served only to amuse her ... which in turn endeared him to her.

He drove straight from Heathrow to see her on his return from his trip to Holland, and she welcomed him with open arms and a chaste—a very chaste—kiss. 'You look tired, Anton. It's almost midnight. You should have gone straight home.' She smiled at him. 'I could have waited one more day. Do you want coffee or a drink?'

'Coffee.' He shrugged his jacket off when she went into the kitchen. He was not tired, he was tense. She might never know what his patience with her was costing him. It was catching up on him, though, and he knew that something would have to give—and soon. If anyone had told him he would be able to behave as he was doing with a woman as desirable as Lorna, he would never have believed it. He had heard it said that love makes one do strange, sometimes impossible things, and he was now finding this out for himself. Ah, but he loved her! And because of that he was coping.

The tension inside him was not caused wholly by the physical strain he was under, it was partly because he could not yet tell her how he felt about her. He would have to wait until the time was right. They had established a relationship built on firm foundations and as time passed it was being added to slowly, brick by brick. But still it was too soon for declarations. She held back from him in more than the physical sense, and he would have to overcome this first before he asked her to marry him. To rush her would only frighten her off.

'Here's your coffee, sir. How did your trip go?'

'Fine. The next one will probably be my last.'

Lorna sat facing him. He was on the settee, which always seemed to shrink in size when Anton was lounging on it. But tonight he wasn't lounging, he wasn't even relaxed, and this was odd. She looked at him closely, feeling worried. Had he come to tell her it was finished between them? 'There's something on your mind, Anton. What is it?'

He just looked at her, unsmiling. 'Have you ever been in love, Lorna?'

The question took her by surprise. 'No.'

He seemed to think about this. 'Then it was a purely physical thing?'

'What? What are you talking about?'

'Stop fencing, Lorna. It's time you told me about it. I know there's something ... I know you've been hurt somewhere along the line. I've asked you to tell me about it several times. Before I came into your life, you had a reputation as a manhater, do you know that?'

She sighed. 'You've been talking to Eve.'

'I had a drink with her before I left for the airport last week. Don't be cross with her, she didn't volunteer anything. I asked her to tell me who you'd been seeing during the year she'd known you, before you met me. She said there was no one. Nobody at all.'

'So?'

'So why? And why did you have a reputation as a manhater?'

She looked directly at him. 'I wasn't aware that I had, but—no, there hasn't been anyone ... any one man.'

'Your relationships in the past have always been casual, short-lived. Is that what you're telling me?'

She didn't answer.

'Look, all I know about you is how you are today. I want you to tell me more. Tell me about your past—all of it. I know about your father's death. Take it from there.'

'You want my life story?' Lorna laughed shortly and then sighed again. She would tell him. She didn't mind telling him. There was no way she would include the incident with Jake Dougan, though. 'It isn't a pretty story.' This was true, even with the omission of Jake's attack.

She told him all there was to tell—with that exception. She did mention Jake, but only in the context of his being the last of the men in her mother's life. 'My mother was thirty-five when she died. She'd been in hospital with bronchial pneumonia and further complications set in. She died in hospital. Cathy and I were taken into care——'

'And what about Jake, this man who'd been living with you?'

'He—he moved on to the next woman, I suppose. I—I never saw him again.'

'Go on.'

'Well, Cathy was in the children's home far longer than I, being so much younger. When I left, I got a job in a shop and lived in a bed-sit. Upstairs there was a man—he was about twenty, I suppose—who did all sorts of casual work. We got on quite well as neighbours. It was his idea that we could set up business together, on the markets. We started with next to nothing, selling cheap clothing. Rejects and seconds mostly. But we built up a fair trade and got regular stalls on three different markets. This was in Manchester. I'd always intended to move to London one day—when Cathy was with me. I knew then what I wanted to do, you see. *Feline* was my goal. Anyway, I was set back when my so-called friend and colleague suddenly did a moonlight——'

'A moonlight?'

'A vanishing act. He took the old van we'd bought, the stock that was in it and our cash float. Oh, it didn't amount to a great deal, but it was a lot in my eyes. I later realised he'd cheated me in another way, too. He'd been pocketing some of the takings instead of putting it into the cashbox. It became obvious to me later. Anyhow, the whole thing set me back.'

'So what did you do?'

'I started again,' she shrugged. 'I already had some savings by then. I spent some of them and carried on. I bought another old van——' She looked up suddenly. 'Come to think of it, that was one good thing that emerged from my experience with my partner—he taught me to drive. Where was I? Yes, I did quite well on the markets, and at night I worked as a waitress. I also sold catalogue stuff, for which I got commission. I saved every single penny.'

'For your goal.'

'For my dream. As soon as I got my sister back we moved to London. We'd planned on running the shop together. We looked all over the place to find suitable premises to rent, but we came to Windsor by accident, really—one day when we'd just gone out for a drive. I loved the place. So did Cathy.'

'So how come Cathy isn't with you now?'

'She was lured into something more glamorous. I suppose it makes sense, considering her looks. I don't think she'd have lasted in the shop, anyway. It was my dream but not hers. Cathy wants more from life than a reasonable living. Before the shop opened, when we were buying stock for it in London, Cathy was offered a job as a model in one of the fashion showrooms.' Lorna's shrug was philosophical then. 'The owner of the place raved about her and she took the job. She worked for him briefly—until she found a better prospect. Eventually she started working for the agency she's with now and—well, soon we'll be seeing her on television. Very soon, come to think of it. End of story.'

It was a long time before Anton said anything. While Lorna had been talking he had remained impassive, his expression showing only interest. Lorna had watched him keenly, looking for expressions of distaste. Never before had she told someone all about herself. And she had told him everything—except the incident of which she was ashamed. That was more than she could bring herself to do.

'I wish you'd say something, Anton. Are you appalled? For one with your background, my past is probably incomprehensible.'

'Appalled?' Now he looked shocked and upset. 'Lorna, I'm proud—of you. You made it. You got what you wanted and you did it the hard way. What else can one do but admire you?'

His vehemence embarrassed her slightly. He was a lovely man, so dear to her. At ease again, she looked at him fondly, smiling. 'You look grave now, Anton. What is it? What's bugging you now?'

'Two questions.'

'Fire away.' She could cope. She felt more confident than she had ever felt with him, and she had always felt reasonably confident with him. That's how he made her feel. She trusted him, too, far more than she had before, even if it wasn't one hundred per cent.

'The young man, your partner. Was there anything between you?'

'Only business. And his cheating me financially.'

He nodded as if he had expected this answer. Then he got up and moved around the room restlessly. 'From all you've told me there doesn't seem to have been room, time, for boy-friends.'

'There wasn't.'

He turned to face her, his hands thrust deep inside his pockets. 'Then that makes my second question unnecessary.'

Lorna looked down at the carpet. 'I'll be twenty-six next month. You must find this incomprehensible, too.'

He sat down again, and as he did so she saw that the tension had gone from his face. 'Nothing is incomprehensible now, my darling. Nothing. Thank you for telling me—for trusting me with this. The mystery is solved. I understand you completely now.'

'You do?'

'Better than you understand yourself, probably.'

'No, I understand myself very well, Anton. Believe me, I try very hard not to be biased, not to judge all men by the behaviour of those my mother got involved with. I do try to keep things in perspective, honestly. Jean wasn't a bad person, I'd hate you to think that. She always did her best for me and Cathy. Really, she didn't stand a chance of living a decent life. She was too soft, too weak. She always got involved with the wrong kind of men. I'm aware of it even though I'll never understand it. I know I'm very different from her. You see, I can keep things in perspective. I'm not really a manhater.'

'I never thought you were,' he smiled. Then, his expression serious, 'You once made a remark which puzzled me . . . you said that in your experience, when there are men in one's life, there's trouble.'

Lorna's smile was wry. 'No doubt you understand that remark now.'

'No, I don't.'

'But——'

'Because there's never been a man in your life.'

'How can you say that? There's been a string of them!'

'No,' he said firmly. 'Think about it. They were in your *mother's* life, not yours.'

The statement took Lorna by surprise. It was a new thought.

'There's never been a man in your life.' Anton repeated it deliberately. 'You were Jean's daughter, naturally her lifestyle affected you. But you were a child; you were in no position to do anything about it. You know you're different from Jean in every possible way—yet what did you do when you reached maturity? You locked yourself up behind your prejudices. You *are* biased. Do you call this living, being sealed up in an exclusively women's world?'

Lorna stared at him, startled. 'You mean *Feline*? I—I never thought of it like that. I—I've never considered things from this angle. I suppose you're right.'

'You don't keep a balance on things. You're biased. And that's illogical.'

'Yes. Yes . . . it is.'

Anton knew a feeling of relief, release. He knew, finally, why she was afraid of him, why she insisted on keeping their dates down to a minimum, why she held back from him in so many ways. 'Lorna, have I succeeded in breaking the bad associations you have with the past, with men in general?'

She laughed at that. 'You're here, aren't you? Let's face it, you are a part of my life now.'

'I've had to fight to be so.'

'I know.'

'And I shall continue to be part of your life. How do you feel about that?'

Lorna didn't need to think about it. 'Glad.' She looked directly at his eyes. 'I'm happy about it.'

Anton smiled inwardly, his relief total. He could tell her now. The time was right now. Furthermore, it was important that he did so. She needed very much to be loved, to *know* she was loved. He watched her closely, carefully, as he told her, 'I love you, Lorna. I've loved you for a long time.'

He wanted to go to her, to take her in his arms, but he made himself stay where he was. He must continue to be patient with her; the look on her face made that painfully clear to him. 'Are you so surprised? Darling, I've tried to show you I love you. I've been trying all along. Think about it.'

'I—I thought——'

'You thought that the past three months have been one long seduction routine.' His smile was wry, almost sad.

Lorna didn't really know what to say. He had tried to show her. In lots of ways he had tried to do that. He loved her. She should have seen it weeks ago. Instead she had allowed her cynicism to dictate to her. She had been wary, waiting for him to lose patience, but he never had. And in a way she had also been testing him, waiting for him to tire of her or grow bored, because deep down inside she could not believe that a man such as he could love a girl like her. But she and Anton were no longer worlds apart. And she knew without doubt that he was sincere.

He came to her then, pulling her gently to her feet. He lifted her face, touching her so lightly, so tenderly she felt a shock ripple through her. 'My darling Lorna, nothing has ever come easily to you, has it? And nothing in your life has been consistent. Not until you opened your shop, and then you made it your only support in life, your only reason for living. Do you see now what I meant when I tried to talk to you about this?'

She looked up at him, nodding, unable to speak for the sudden rush of tenderness she was feeling towards him.

His fingers were still cupping her face, his eyes sombre and anxious as he looked into hers. 'You've never trusted before. You've never trusted anyone but yourself. But I want you to trust me now. I won't try to rush you into anything you're not ready for, I promise you. We'll just continue as we are until you learn to trust me completely, until you believe that I love you absolutely. For the moment, I don't expect anything from you, Lorna. You mustn't feel obliged to do or say anything.'

Lorna couldn't have spoken if she had wanted to. For the moment, he'd said. For the moment all she wanted to do was to touch him, to hold him, to feel his lips upon hers.

They kissed as they had never kissed before. It began lightly, gently, each having the need to taste, to savour the moment, the communication which went far beyond the physical.

At Lorna's instigation the kiss deepened, changing to one of intensity, hunger. Anton's mouth was probing, exploring, exciting in its sensuality. She lifted her head, arching against him as his lips trailed down the smooth skin of her throat. His own excitement spurred her on and she made no protest when his hands moved under her clothes, trailing lightly over her breasts.

She knew neither panic nor fear. The woman, the passion in her was finally released. Her arms closed possessively around the broadness of his back, her lips once more seeking his. She moved slowly against him, unable to get close enough, and when he moaned softly against her lips she touched him in such a way that he could not doubt her willingness to be one with him.

He lifted her bodily, scooping her high into his arms as he carried her to the settee, and Lorna's eyes closed involuntarily. Terror struck her like a physical blow, suddenly. This was so reminiscent of . . . She fought it. She tried so hard to fight back against her fear, knowing with her intellect that this was Anton, *Anton*.

Her eyes came open as he laid her down, still holding her as he knelt beside her. 'Oh, God, no! *No!*' The words tore from her of their own volition and she slapped his hands from her body, pushing him away from her with all the strength she had.

The silence screamed in her ears. Anton said nothing. Absolutely nothing. She would never know what was written on his face because she couldn't look at him.

She just lay where she was, trembling, her heart hammering inside her chest, her face flushed with shame at her own behaviour. That was all she was aware of. That and his presence.

And his silence.

The silence was broken when she heard the door closing softly as he left. Lorna covered her face with her hands, her body shaking with uncontrollable sobs.

CHAPTER NINE

It was over between her and Anton. It was, she told herself, just as well.

How long she had lain there, she didn't know. Her watch told her it was five a.m. But what time had he left? Not that it mattered. What mattered was that he would not come back. She was sure he wouldn't come back.

Lorna struggled into a sitting position, trying to gather enough energy to go to bed. At least she would be able to sleep late. Tomorrow—today—was Sunday. Again she told herself it would be better if he kept away from her. She would not go after him. For his sake it would be better to finish it now. He deserved better than this.

She got up at noon and took a hot bath, slipped into jeans and a sweater and went out for a walk. It was with a mild sense of shock that she realised she'd left the door of the shop unlocked the previous night. The burglar alarm hadn't been set.

It was a beautiful day, cool and crisp, and in the air there was the feeling of spring. She headed towards Windsor Great Park, and it was only when she walked past Eve's offices that she remembered that she and Anton had been invited to Eve's house for dinner that night. She had forgotten to tell Anton.

Lorna only stayed out for an hour. She headed for home because she was cold. But she didn't want to stay in. Maybe she would go for a drive. As she turned the corner, she stopped in her tracks. Anton's car was parked in front of her shop and he was sitting in the driver's seat, smoking one of his occasional cigarettes.

The acceleration of her heartbeat made her smile at

herself as she walked quickly towards him. Of course he
was back. He'd said he loved her, hadn't he?

When she saw the look on his face, however, she was
filled with dread. He looked—almost grey. If she had
thought him tense last night it was nothing compared to
the way he looked now. His face was taut, his eyes lit
with anger and high in his jaw there was a muscle
working in a steady rhythm.

Lorna stood at the front of the car, almost
mesmerised as he came towards her and gripped her
arm so tightly that a stab of pain shot through her.
Dear God, she hadn't expected this! Never before had
she seen him even remotely angry ... but *this*?
'Anton—don't! Please ... I'm sorry! What else can I
say?' She shrank from him, trying to free her arm.

He did not slacken his hold. His eyes closed briefly
and he seemed to be having difficulty forming his
words. 'It's not you, Lorna. It's all right. Open the
door.'

She did as he said, confused now. If she was not the
object of his anger then who, or what, was the cause of
it? They went upstairs in silence and Lorna sat on the
edge of a chair, her eyes following him as he stalked
about the room. After a moment he flung his jacket on
the settee and turned to face her. 'Jake Dougan.' He
spat out the words. 'Jake Dougan. Why, *why* didn't you
tell me? Why did you lie to me?'

Lorna's mouth opened and closed again. 'I . . .' Her
mind was spinning with questions, protests, fear. Cathy!
There was only one person in the world who could have
told him about Jake. 'I didn't lie, Anton. I——'

'You can lie by omission. It's just as effective!'

She closed her eyes, stunned by the volume of his
voice. For the moment she felt as if she didn't know
him at all. She opened her eyes as she felt his hand
brush lightly over her shoulder. Then he dropped on to
the settee, his face relaxing slightly. 'I'm not angry with
you, Lorna. I just wish I could get my hands on that
bastard!'

He was up again, his fingers raking through his hair. Lorna relaxed against the cushions, feeling drained but relieved. She must let him give vent to his anger. She understood it only too well.

She sat, grim-faced, listening as he swore, making no attempt to stop him. What she had told him last night about Jake's disappearance had been the truth. Jake had disappeared after his attempted rape. The neighbours to whom Lorna had gone running had called the police—but Jake had already gone. The flat was empty. How he had managed this in his drunken state, where he had gone, Lorna didn't know. The police never found him. It was as if Jake Dougan had never existed.

No doubt Cathy had told Anton this; no doubt this piece of information was adding to his anger. 'It was a long time ago, Anton. I'm over it now.'

'Like hell you're over it!'

'Please, please stop shouting. You're making me nervous. I—I'll make some tea.'

He was composed when she emerged from the kitchen. He was by no means his usual self, but he had calmed down sufficiently to talk. 'When—how did you find my sister?'

'She's in the phone book, remember? I spent two hours with her this morning. She told me everything you told me last night. *Plus* that which you omitted!' He sighed, long and hard. 'It's odd. Some time ago, I had considered the possibility that you'd had a bad experience sexually. But I never dreamt you'd been beaten and raped when you were thirteen years old!'

'I wasn't beaten, as you put it. Nor was I raped. Cathy was exaggerating—or you are.'

Anton threw up his hands. 'I don't see how you can be so calm about it!'

'I've told you, I've lived with it for twelve years. It's past, gone. And damn Cathy for telling you. Damn her for her interference! She had no right——' She broke off, smiling humourlessly. 'This is where we came in, eh, you and I? Was this some sort of retaliation on Cathy's part? I suppose she was getting back at me for interfering in her business.'

'Don't be hard on her. Cathy was the only person I could think of who might be able to throw some light on your—behaviour. I insisted she told me everything she knew. She was acting from the best motives.'

'That doesn't excuse——'

'It doesn't excuse you,' he said firmly. 'You should have told me yourself. You should have told me weeks ago, months ago. I'd have understood so much more. Oh, come here, Lorna. Come and sit by me. I want to hold you.'

She went to him, wordlessly, leaving the tea untouched. Anton wanted to hold her and she wanted, very much, to be held. She went trustingly into his arms, resting her head against his shoulder. 'I—I'm sure I would have told you one day.'

He smoothed her hair from her forehead, kissing her lightly as he did so. 'Cathy said you were ashamed of it, Lorna. I've never heard anything so ridiculous. You were innocent, defenceless.'

That was true enough. Lorna said nothing. She felt exhausted, relieved. He knew everything there was to know about her now and he still loved her. She loved him, too. For his constancy, his patience, his tenderness, his strength. 'I love you, Anton.'

She said it quietly because the words were alien to her. The emotion was new to her. If she had started to love him before today, she had not admitted it to herself. But she couldn't deny it now.

He tilted her face up to his so he might see what was in her eyes. 'Then why so sad?' He was smiling, his own eyes telling her of his pleasure. 'There's nothing to worry about now. Nothing and no one will hurt you again. No, don't move away from me. Stay here, stay in my arms.' He rested her head against his shoulder, holding her firmly but gently against him. 'We'll take it slowly, darling. Just get used to being here, where you belong.'

'I—Cathy thinks I should see a psychiatrist.'

'Nonsense! Everything will happen in its own good time. Trust me, Lorna. Now I know the facts, I can cope. We'll take it easy, little by little.' He looked down at her, his smile roguish because she was blushing at his suggestions. 'In future I will be doing exactly what you've been suspecting me of, seduction by stages——'

'Hush!' She put a finger over his lips, embarrassed but a little amused. 'That'll really test your patience!'

He bit lightly on her finger, holding it between his teeth as he spoke, his eyes dancing with laughter. 'But think of the end reward!'

They sat quietly for a long time. Lorna's eyes closed and she revelled in the feel of his arms around her, the clean masculine smell of him, his warmth and his love.

'I'm hungry,' he said at length. 'Let's go out and eat.'

'Oh, that reminds me!' Lorna got to her feet. 'We're eating with Eve and Julian tonight. Okay?'

'Fine. Dining out or dining in?'

'In. At Eve's.'

'Then we'd better make it a light lunch,' he grinned. 'You know what Eve's like!'

It was just as well they had had a light lunch. Eve was a superb cook and an excellent hostess. She had gone to a lot of trouble on the previous occasions they had dined at her home, and tonight was no exception.

'Eve, that was . . .' Anton paused, drained his glass and made an expansive gesture with his free arm. 'What can I say? What can I say? Superb!'

'My dear Anton, I think the fact that you've had two helpings of everything says it all for you!' Eve smiled, bowing her head. 'Thank you, kind sir.'

'Will you keep this up after you're married?' Lorna asked, straight-faced.

'She'd better!' Julian protested. 'Otherwise I shall sue her for misrepresentation.'

Anton shook his head. 'Who'd marry a lawyer?'

'Me.' The declaration came simultaneously as Eve and Julian reached for each other's hand.

'Look at them!' Lorna teased. 'Hey, you two, there's no sign of wedding nerves yet. How come? It isn't far away now.'

'I know, I know,' Eve laughed. 'The nerves are there, all right—every time the wedding is mentioned. Like now!' She looked heavenward.

Lorna wasn't sure whether her friend was joking. The one thing she was sure of was that she wouldn't like to be the bride at such a wedding. She would be overwhelmed. She was overwhelmed just hearing about it, thinking about it. There would be hundreds of guests. The wedding was to take place in St George's, Hanover Square, and the reception would be held in an exclusive London club of which Sir Michael was a member. It would be a society affair on a grand scale, and although it was only a month away, Lorna hadn't given any thought as to what she would wear.

'Have you found a house yet?' Anton was asking. 'It's easier said than done, isn't it?'

'Oh, we've decided not to bother,' Julian told him. 'I meant to tell you last week, when I came to see how your place is coming along. We're going to live here for a while, until Eve gives up work. We'll start looking again as soon as she's pregnant.'

Lorna and Anton exchanged looks, grinning, and while he managed to withhold his comments, Lorna could not. 'Eve? What's all this? I thought you wanted to carry on working...'

'We-ell, Julian thinks——'

'What's all this about starting a family...?'

'Julian thinks——'

'Julian thinks?' Lorna wouldn't let go. 'And what about you?'

'I'm thirty.' Her simple answer put a stop to Lorna's teasing. 'I haven't got all that much time to spare.'

When the two girls went into the kitchen to fetch the coffee, Eve put her hand on Lorna's arm, her face serious. 'It's what I want, Lorna. I want Julian's children and I don't want to wait too long.'

'Hey, I was only teasing!'

'I know, but—wow, when I think how different I used to be only a year ago! My thinking has changed, I've changed.'

'Me too.' Lorna nodded in understanding. 'When I think about how much *I've* changed during the past few months!' She glanced in the direction of the dining room. 'It's been a . . . a very subtle process.' And it hasn't finished yet, she added to herself.

She turned back to find Eve grinning like a Cheshire cat. 'I'm not one to say I told you so——'

'Then don't!'

'But I told you so. You do realise you're next?'

'What does that mean?' Lorna frowned, having no idea what she meant.

'Oh, come on, Lorna! You're too far gone to keep up any pretence. For the altar, you idiot, for the altar!'

'Wrong,' Lorna said crisply. 'We're perfectly happy with the status quo.' It was the truth. Well, almost.

Eve frowned, unsure whether Lorna meant what she was saying.

'By the way, it's my birthday next Saturday.' Lorna changed the subject to something more comfortable. 'I'll do the honours. Can you and Julian make it on Sunday? It'll be just the four of us.'

'Lovely! Yes, of course we can make it.'

'It'll have to be Sunday because there's no way I could cope with a dinner party after a Saturday afternoon in the shop.'

Eve picked up the tray of coffee cups, still curious about Lorna's attitude. 'The shop still comes first, Lorna? I mean . . . before anything else?'

'Too right.' Lorna picked up the coffee percolator. 'After you, Eve.' She gestured towards the dining room, smiling at the frown on Eve's face.

Anton and Julian had transferred to the living room, and it was only as Lorna walked in there that something dropped into place. 'Just a minute!' She plonked the percolator down as everyone turned to look at her. 'Julian, didn't you say something about going to see Anton's house last week?'

'Yes,' Julian said innocently. 'Why?' He looked curiously at Anton. 'Shouldn't I have said that? What gives?'

'I'll tell you what gives!' said Lorna, glaring at the Dutchman. 'I haven't been invited, but it looks as though everyone else has!'

'You're banned,' Anton said coolly. 'But only until it's finished. I've told you, you can see it when it's finished.'

'What is all this?' Julian asked. 'What am I missing?'

'You've put your foot in it, darling,' Eve informed him. 'I told you ages ago that Anton won't let Lorna near the place until he's had it furnished and whatnot.'

'And why is it taking so long?' The question came from Lorna.

'Well, he's knocked down a few walls...' Julian thought he was defending Anton and succeeded only in making things worse. Eve stuck a coffee cup in his hand and told him to shut up.

'Doesn't Lorna know anything?' Julian was winding her up, she realised that at his next words. 'I mean, hasn't Anton told you about the woman who's moved in with him?'

'No.' Lorna would not rise to it.

'Or the man?'

'I happen to know Anton isn't that way inclined.'

Eve was laughing her head off. 'Stop it, Julian! Stop mixing things.'

Anton was watching Lorna. 'Now you don't know what to believe, do you?'

Lorna wouldn't answer him. She spoke directly to Julian. 'Let me explain: Anton wanted me to help him with his new house. I refused. Now he's acting out of pique. That's what it's all about!'

'Is that what you think?' Anton threw back his head, roaring with laughter. 'Shame on you! Anyhow, the bit about the man and woman is true. I've got myself a cook/housekeeper and a handyman/gardener—a married couple. They're living in the staff cottage at the back of the main building.'

'Oh! Well, I'm glad to hear it.' Lorna was glad to hear it. She was also surprised, though she couldn't imagine why she was having either of these reactions.

CHAPTER TEN

'I'M sorry, I've got too much to do.' Lorna must have said these words once a month for the past—well, almost every month since she had opened *Feline*. Paul, the representative who fancied his chances, had asked her yet again if he could take her to lunch. She had lost count of the number of times she had given him the brush-off, of the number of times he'd ignored it.

If she had not met Anton, if she had not become far more tolerant as a result of that, she would have put Paul in his place with one short, sharp sentence. And she would have done it months ago. But she had changed in so many ways since knowing Anton. Life, her points of view, her attitudes were different now. Quite why this was so, she wasn't sure. In fact, she wasn't altogether certain that it was a good thing.

Nevertheless she gave Paul a brilliant smile and put him in his place fairly gently. 'Give it up, Paul. The answer is no and it will always be no.'

He grinned at her. 'Now you can't blame a man for trying. Faint heart and all that.'

'Yes, yes.' Lorna waved a dismissive arm as she saw him to the door. 'Goodbye, Paul. See you next month.'

She went into the stockroom to help Dulcie with the boxes she was unpacking. 'He did it again,' she said indignantly. 'Honestly! But I made myself very clear today.'

'I heard,' Dulcie laughed. 'Why don't you just tell him you're committed elsewhere?'

Lorna looked up quickly. 'Who says I'm committed elsewhere?'

'Aren't you?'

Lorna's hand reached up to touch the pearls she was wearing. Anton had given them to her for her birthday, and she hadn't wanted to accept them. They were obviously wildly expensive.

'Anton, I can't accept these. They're so—so . . .'

'So appropriate for the dress you're wearing.' He had silenced her with a kiss, taken the pearls from their dark velvet box and ordered her to turn around while he fastened them in place.

The memory came to her unbidden. That had been several weeks ago and until today Lorna had only worn the pearls twice, on her birthday and at Eve's wedding. Eve and Julian were in the Caribbean, well into the second week of their long honeymoon. Their wedding had been beautiful, out of this world, and Eve had never looked as lovely as she did on that day.

'Lorna?'

'What? Oh—sorry.' She let her hand drop. Dulcie's smile was all-knowing, too much so. Lorna was irritated by it, and yet she could not blame the older woman for her assumptions. Dulcie made no secret of her admiration for Anton—purely as a prospective husband for her boss, of course. At least, that was all Lorna thought it was!

'No,' Lorna said at length. 'I'm not *committed*.'

Dulcie almost sniffed at that. 'Lorna, if you ever consider selling the shop, will you give me first refusal?'

'Selling the shop?' Lorna just stared at her. 'Dulcie, I've no intention of doing such a thing. Really! I'm——' She broke off, her eyebrows raised. 'I didn't realise you liked the business *that* much. You mean you'd like a shop of your own?'

'This one, perhaps. Of course I'd have to discuss it with my husband but ... well ... the idea rather appeals to me.'

Not *my* shop, Lorna thought. Give up *Feline*? The woman must be out of her mind!

The telephone rang then and Lorna reached for it, smiling as she heard the familiar deep voice. 'Hey, what is this?' Anton was supposed to be coming to take her to lunch—which was the only reason she had decided to wear the pearls while she was working. He was phoning to cancel the arrangement. 'Am I losing my charms or something?'

'You must be joking.' There was a smile in his voice. 'I haven't finished discovering them yet ... not *all* of them!'

'Anton!' Lorna turned away, worried that Dulcie might be able to hear what he was saying.

She kept her conversation as brief as possible because it was obvious Dulcie wouldn't leave the room until or unless she was asked to. 'So when will I see you?'

'Tonight. I'll pick you up at seven sharp. Will that give you enough time to get ready?'

'For what?'

'A dinner party. A private affair.'

'Where?'

'Here. At the house. It's ready for inspection.'

'Great! You've certainly kept me waiting long enough.'

'There's no answer to that.' There was laughter now.

'Yes, I'll be ready.' Lorna was getting more uncomfortable by the minute. Bother Dulcie and her curiosity!

'There will be four of us in all,' Anton went on.

'Oh! I thought—I mean, you said——'

'A private affair? It will be, my darling. See you!'

He hung up before she could say anything else— which was probably as well, eavesdroppers considered.

As soon as she had finished for the day Lorna took a quick bath and put on fresh make-up, pondering over what to wear. She brushed her hair until it shone and pushed at the soft, coppery waves with her fingers, counting herself lucky that her hair, at least, never presented her with a problem.

Who were the other two guests dining at Anton's tonight? If she knew, it might influence her choice of clothes. It wasn't Eve and Julian, so who else might it be? Sir Michael and Lady Summers, perhaps? She should have asked Anton whether she should dress up or be reasonably casual.

For someone who owned a ladieswear shop, Lorna's wardrobe was not extensive ... but there was a jersey dress downstairs which would solve her immediate dilemma. It was emerald green, the colour which suited her most, and while it was strictly speaking a day dress, the addition of the right accessories and jewellery would make the necessary transformation.

Anton looked pleased when he saw she was wearing the pearls. He gave an exaggerated bow as he held the car door open for her. 'You look . . .' He leaned close to her as she sat, whispering in her ear.

She giggled as he walked round to the driving seat. 'Anton, in no way could this dress be described as sexy! You've got sex on the brain, do you know that?'

'It isn't the dress so much as the way you wear it.'

Only then did it register that he was wearing a casual jacket and slacks, an open-necked shirt. 'Unless you're changing for dinner, I've overdone it. Who's joining us, anyway? I forgot to ask you how I should dress tonight.'

'Oh, the other two aren't fussy. They'll like you no matter what you're wearing.'

'Darling, who are these people? Do I know them?'

Anton shook his head and Lorna gave up. He seemed reluctant to talk about them, so she'd just have to wait and see. When they turned into the driveway of Anton's house, the mystery was solved. They hadn't got as far as the house when two full-grown Alsatians came bounding towards the car. 'Our company for this evening,' Anton smiled. 'Leo and Wolf.'

'Oh, Anton, they're gorgeous!' Lorna laughed delightedly. 'Do you know, I'd forgotten about them. You haven't mentioned them for ages! When did you get them back?'

'Three days ago. I thought I'd keep it as a surprise.' He clamped a hand on her shoulder, suddenly. 'Don't open the door. Wolf is a suspicious devil and Leo's

already made himself king of the castle. I'll just have a
word with them before I introduce you.'

She laughed at his choice of words, but she could see
what he meant. Leo and Wolf were no doubt
formidable guard-dogs. They also knew who was the
boss. Lorna watched as Anton gave them a moment to
enthuse over his return then he stilled them with a one-
word command and let Lorna out of the car.

She patted them, even cuddled them, without any
fear or misgivings—or a thought for her clothes—
laughing at the speed with which their tails were
wagging.

'You're in!' Anton told her with a smile. 'They're
looking good, aren't they?'

'Yes. But I'll bet they're glad to be out of
quarantine.'

Her second surprise was the cook/housekeeper who
opened the front door as they approached. Lorna had
seen her somewhere before, she knew she had, but she
couldn't for the life of her think where.

'Mrs Gray—Miss Stewart.' Anton made the introduction and Lorna said what she'd just been thinking.

'At Mr Karel's house.' Mrs Gray was smiling,
remembering Lorna very clearly. 'Last September or
October, I think it was. When you called to see Mr Anton.'

'Ah, yes! Yes, of course.' Lorna and Anton
exchanged looks and she saw his barely suppressed
amusement. She had a mental picture of herself
standing on Karel's doorstep talking to Mrs Gray, then
waiting in that awful living room of his, then screaming
at Anton . . . And look how much has happened since
then, she thought. Look how far the wheel of fate has
turned . . .

'I've pinched Mrs Gray from my cousin,' Anton was
saying. 'She and her husband have made themselves
quite at home here, haven't you Mrs Gray?'

'In the cottage.' The housekeeper looked delighted.
'Oh, it's beautiful here! So quiet! And Mr Anton has
been so kind in——'

'Now, now, come on,' Anton cut her off. 'We'll start with the kitchen, shall we? After you, Mrs Gray.'

Lorna's guided tour started in the kitchen, and she barely noticed the smell of something delicious in the making. She was astonished. From the outside she had noticed no change. The house and grounds looked just as they had when she had first seen them. Then, the inside of the house had been lovely as it was—albeit empty except for carpets and curtains. But Anton had made drastic changes. In the hall and kitchen, at least.

'It's beautiful!' Lorna looked round in amazement. Everything was spanking new, all the units and cupboards were matching, beautifully fitted and finished.

'It's functional, too.' Anton put in. 'I'll let you do the honours, Mrs Gray.'

The housekeeper showed Lorna everything from the smallest gadget to the dishwasher which looked like a cupboard from the outside. Lorna showed an interest in everything, impressed by Mrs Gray's enthusiasm as much as anything else.

'I don't remember the room being so big.' She frowned, trying to remember what it had looked like before. It had been modern and smart as it was, but . . .

'One of the walls I knocked down,' Anton explained. 'This part of it used to be the laundry room, remember? What used to be the downstairs study has now been designated for that purpose. Through there.'

They took a quick look at the room next door, the dogs trailing after them, then left Mrs Gray to get on with dinner. Wolf and Leo were ordered to stay as they went upstairs. 'They're not allowed up here,' Anton explained as he took Lorna's arm. 'You won't see a vast difference up here, except for the decorating.'

Apart from the master bedroom, that was true. Lorna followed him from room to room, nodding in approval. 'You've furnished the guest rooms, too.'

'Of course. We'll be having a housewarming party

soon, darling. But that will be your department. You can decide who'll sleep over.'

His words made her uneasy. *We*, he'd said. We'll be having a housewarming . . .

'Good heavens!' Lorna's eyebrows went up in surprise as they stepped into the bathroom en suite to the master bedroom. 'That bath! It's big enough for . . .'

'Two.' Anton caught hold of her by the waist, his arms tightening as she tried to wriggle free.

'Kinky, are you?' Lorna laughed at him and stopped wriggling.

'Lonely,' he amended. 'Don't you think it a very civilised idea, communal bathing? The Japanese do it all the time.'

'I don't know about communal.' She pouted, waiting, wanting to be kissed. 'I wouldn't mind just the two of us . . .'

She got what she wanted and it went on for a long, long time. 'Hey, enough of this.' Anton let go of her reluctantly. 'Dinner's almost ready.'

Lorna slid her arms around his neck, pressing the length of her body against his. 'So am I.' She brushed his lips lightly with her own. 'Simmering, you might say.' Her laughter was soft, seductive as she teased him with her closeness.

'Darling Lorna, there's a time and a place . . .'

By way of reply she slid her hands under his jacket and pulled the shirt from his slacks at the back, watching his eyes close as she started caressing his skin. The size of him, the very power of him was in itself exciting to her now. 'Forget the almost,' she murmured. 'I'm ready, darling. The time is now and . . . there's a double bed in there. Why don't I stay the night?'

'It's polite to wait until you're asked.' Anton failed to maintain an admonitory tone. His voice was thick with arousal and the way she was talking was doing nothing for his powers of control . . . not to mention what she was doing to him now. 'Lorna——'

She slid one of her hands from his back and let it trail

along his thigh until she was touching him shamelessly and loving every minute of it.

He kissed her hungrily, unable to resist. 'You're a wanton. That's what I've turned you into.'

'Tonight, Anton . . .' She gasped softly as his mouth came down on hers, exploring her mouth and probing slowly, suggestively, until she was aching with her need of him.

They had come closer and closer to this over the past few weeks. Tonight she wanted him to make love to her completely, fully. Her fears had been gradually worn away by Anton each and every time he had taken her into his arms and led her slowly, gently, to this readiness. And he had done it with such exquisite tenderness that even the memory of those times were enough to set her pulses racing. But there was no such tenderness from him now, there was only passion. Lorna was equal to it, more than eager to return it.

Anton kissed her hungrily, leaving her in no doubt of his intention. He knew she needed him now as much as he needed her. But for the moment he eased her away from him. Oh yes, they would consummate their love tonight. This evening, this night was planned down to the last detail. He had not known quite when it would be, but he had thought about it, prepared for it, for a long time. 'Darling, we must go downstairs. How are you going to feel if Mrs Gray comes looking for us?'

'Highly embarrassed. Is she likely to?'

'You know she isn't,' he grinned. 'I'm just trying to get you to behave yourself—temporarily, of course. Now go on.' He smacked her playfully on the bottom as she turned away. 'You'll just have to wait a while longer.'

'Hey! That's—that *was*—my line!' Lorna protested saucily, turning to look at him. She laughed and linked her arm through his, clearing her throat noisily. 'Anton, I think we'd better stay in here for a minute or two. Er—give you time to compose yourself. We'll—er—talk about the bathroom. Have you—Oh, *stop* that!'

She laughed hysterically as he started tickling her. 'Stop it! I can't bear it. Wait, wait, seriously, I want to say something!'

He let go of her and she gasped for breath, still laughing.

'Well?'

'This bathroom. It's gorgeous! And bigger. Another wall?'

'The second and last,' he nodded. 'What used to be the linen store, that little room next door, is now part of our bathroom.'

The uneasiness Lorna had experienced earlier came back at once. *Our* bathroom, he'd said. Was it just his way of speaking because she would be spending a good deal of time here, or was she going to be the last person to know what everyone else had apparently been taking for granted? Eve, Julian, Dulcie—even Cathy had hinted at it when Lorna had had a quick lunch with her a couple of weeks earlier. And Cathy should have known better.

If there was any doubt remaining in Lorna's mind, it was removed when Anton showed her the last room of the house, downstairs. He stepped in front of her, smiling. 'The last surprise.' He opened the door for her and let her go in first.

She took in the sight, the atmosphere of the room in one swift, sweeping glance. Tears sprang instantly to her eyes, she was so very touched by what she saw. She was also saddened by what it meant. Anton was going to propose to her, probably tonight.

It was a big living room, forty feet long and almost as wide. It overlooked the gardens and the open spaces beyond. She watched Anton as he went to close the curtains, aware of the violent and nervous thumping of her heart.

The carpet was a deep rose colour, very similar to the one in her own flat except that it was a superior quality. In the stone fireplace, which had not existed before, there was a coal fire burning, making an attractive focal

point in the room. The furniture was not unlike her
own, either, except that it was bigger and there was
more of it, in keeping with a room this size. It certainly
had the same feeling about it.

Lorna remembered only too clearly describing to
Anton the tables and lamps she intended to get for her
flat, as soon as she could afford them . . . and here they
were. The one thing she would never have thought of
buying was the grand piano which occupied a corner,
but that too was aesthetically pleasing, with its rich,
lovingly polished wood. No doubt it was something
Anton had owned for some time, something he had had
shipped over from Holland. There was an escritoire and
one or two other items which had probably come from
his Dutch home, and these, too, were right for the
room. There was a television, the only thing which
smacked of modernity, but even that was softened by its
dark wood cabinet.

Lastly, and most touching of all, were the bowls of
freshly-cut flowers on the coffee tables.

The room was not without a decidedly masculine
stamp, the contribution of Anton's personality, shown
not least by the paintings on the walls. Nevertheless she
could not deny for one moment that the room, the
atmosphere, had been designed—created—to please
her.

The last surprise, he had said. Well, it was certainly a
surprise.

Anton was beside her now, looking at her expectantly,
waiting for her comments. She simply did not know
what to say. Because she had no idea how else she could
handle the situation she made an attempt at flippancy.
But even as she smiled she was well aware that her eyes
were bright with tears. 'It's—what can I say? You—
you've managed to make it very cottage-like.'

She had used the same words Anton had used when
he had first seen her living room, but her attempt at
lightness didn't come off. He slipped his arm around
her waist and stood for a moment, saying nothing. And

he obviously misunderstood why there were tears in her eyes.

'Why don't you pour us a drink?' he said at length. 'I'll just tell Mrs Gray we'll be eating shortly and I'll put the dogs out for the night.'

'They—don't sleep indoors?'

'At this time of year? Outside, in kennels.' He laughed at the look on her face. 'They're quite warm and comfortable enough, don't look so worried!'

The last thing Lorna was worrying about was where Leo and Wolf spent their nights. At that moment she was worried only about how she was going to get through the rest of the evening. She poured herself a brandy and drank it straight off. Maybe she was mistaken? No. No way. Anton was his cool, usual self, but she couldn't fool herself into thinking she was mistaken. He was going to ask her to marry him, and marriage was not, it absolutely was not, what she wanted. Not even to Anton Van der Buren—regardless of the fact that she loved him.

CHAPTER ELEVEN

SHE sank into one of the armchairs, only to get up again at once. It was certainly out of character, and whether or not it was also idiotic considering her lack of food, Lorna didn't stop to think. She poured herself another drink, a large one, and was half way through it when Anton came back.

She handed him a glass and sat next to him when he patted the cushion on the settee. The brandy had seared its path warmly into the heart of her, and it helped enormously. But she was not really a drinker and she was already slightly giddy but far, far from giggly. All in all she managed to appear as relaxed and natural as Anton had taught her to be with him, as she always was with him. They talked about day-to-day matters, of the postcards they had received from Eve and Julian, who were taking a four-week honeymoon. Then Mrs Gray announced that dinner was ready and the evening progressed as smoothly as it should, with Lorna coping very well in the circumstances.

Towards the end of their meal it occurred to her that it might in fact be better to pre-empt Anton, to stop him from asking the question. But what if she *were* mistaken? What an idiot she would make of herself—and how embarrassing it would be for him!

'You're very quiet all of a sudden.' Anton picked up the wine bottle and she shook her head.

'No more wine, thanks. Sorry if I'm quiet. This—this evening has come as quite a shock to me.' She said it with just the right amount of seriousness.

'A shock?' His frown was chased away by a smile. 'You didn't really think I'd kept you away out of pique, did you?'

She shrugged. 'There was a possibility. After all, you

166

did want to give me carte blanche in furnishing this place.' Her own words rang in her ears and she reached unconsciously to touch the pearls at her neck. Why hadn't she realised then, months ago, that marriage was on the cards? She had been blind to it because it simply had not figured in her thinking. She had been concerned with very different matters at that particular time ... such as her resolve to see him only occasionally ...

They took coffee in the living room so Mrs Gray could clear their débris before retiring to her cottage for the evening. She popped in to wish them goodnight, obviously very happy with her new position.

Lorna glanced at her watch. 'Anton, would you mind very much if we have the telly on for a while? A little later, I mean. Cathy's going to be on. They're showing the first in that series of commercials she was working on and I promised we'd look out for it.'

We would look out for it? She was doing it herself now!

'Of course I don't mind. We can't miss that. After all, she's responsible for bringing us together.' He saw, and misinterpreted, the swift look she gave him. He held up a silencing hand. 'All right, she's only partly responsible. I haven't forgotten Karel's part in it.'

The wheel of fate again, Lorna thought. Everything seemed to have gone full circle, she was feeling that strongly tonight. But there would be no accidental pregnancy for Lorna. Common sense was as dominant in her as ever (or was it her instinct for self-preservation?) and she had seen Doctor Smith a while ago.

'You've gone quiet again, Lorna.'

She didn't tell him what was going through her mind. She had already told him about her visit to the doctor. 'I could use another cup of coffee.' She handed her cup to him, but it didn't get her anywhere.

'You know where the kitchen is,' he grinned. 'Bring me one while you're in there.'

They never saw Cathy's television début. Anton followed her into the kitchen because he couldn't keep his hands off her any longer. Lorna didn't want him to. She laughed as she saw him come into the kitchen, recognising the look in his eyes, and dodged out of his grasp as he reached for her. They were about to become lovers, and life with Anton as both friend and lover was something she certainly did want.

She squealed as he caught her, his very touch sending shock waves through her body. She could tease him mercilessly now, deliberately and unconcernedly, because there was no longer anything to worry about.

'So this is how it's going to be!' His eyes crinkled with laughter as she jerked her head away, avoiding his kiss. He muttered something unintelligible.

'What was that all about?'

'Loosely translated,' he said, playing along with her for the moment, 'I said I can see I'm going to have to tame you now!'

'Oh, yes?' she goaded. 'And how do you propose to do that?'

'Like this.' He said it very, very quietly, and Lorna sucked her breath in sharply, feeling every nerve in her body tingling in anticipation. She couldn't keep it up; as his arms closed around her she was already reaching for him, her fingers sliding through the dark blond thickness of his hair.

Anton picked her up effortlessly, kissing her as he held her high in his arms. As he carried her into the living room, she laughed softly. 'You're going in the wrong direction!' She was pointing upwards, but he just laughed at her as he set her down.

'Come here you impatient, beautiful wanton!' He pulled her next to him as he sat, his arms closing around her.

And then it came. All traces of laughter disappeared from his eyes and he looked at her with that familiar openness she had grown to love. He pulled away slightly, taking both of her hands in his. 'Lorna, I have no more surprises in store. What I'm going to say now will not be a surprise to you. Will you marry me, darling? Marry me and share my life so that . . .'

Anton's voice trailed off. He would never forget this moment as long as he lived. *He had not anticipated this.* She didn't need to give him her answer. He had seen it in her eyes in the moment during which she had looked at him before sharply turning her head away. He sat perfectly still. For long seconds his mind refused to function.

He had, he thought, given her plenty of time. For months he had waited, prepared her, for this. And now . . . He put a hand under her chin, turning her to face him. As he did so the tears on her cheeks trickled on to his fingertips. Her unhappiness wrenched at his heart. She didn't want to hurt him and that, at least, was something. But he already knew that she loved him. She had told him so several times. 'Why, Lorna? You're in love with me, so why this?'

For the life of her, she couldn't speak. She moved away from him, fumbling for the tissues in her handbag. She stood with her back to him, not wanting to see the look in his eyes. How could she begin to explain herself? But she had to, she knew. She had to make him understand. She owed him that. 'Anton, I . . . until I stepped into this room tonight, I'd no idea that you . . .' She put cool hands to a face that was flushed, moist with tears. 'It—just isn't what I want. Marriage is so—so final. I can't handle that. I can't handle the responsibility. I've spent so many years having no one but myself to worry about. I've fought to come as far as I have in life. I want, need, my independence. *Feline* has——'

'I haven't asked you to give up your shop, Lorna. I know what it means to you, what it represents. I'll admit that I would have wanted you to, in time. I thought that in time you would be able to let it go, that you would want to let go of it. Lorna——'

'No, don't.' She turned to face him. 'Don't say any more. You'll probably never understand.'

'Please let me finish,' he said quietly. 'Believe me, I'm not going to try to talk you into anything. That would be pointless, foolish.'

'But you said that before,' she whispered. 'You said you wouldn't try to rush me into anything I——'

'Rush you? Darling, it's been five months!'

'And that's such a short time . . .'

Anton did not finish what he wanted to say, not just then. He got to his feet. 'I'll take you home.'

'Home? But I——'

'I'll get your coat.'

He said it in such a way that she had no choice but to comply. Lorna picked up her bag and followed him to the hall. There was so much more that she wanted to say. She did not want it to be over between them. But it was impossible to talk to him now. He had withdrawn from her, and it was very understandable.

They drove in silence, the atmosphere in the car strained to the point of unpleasantness. At least, that was how it seemed to her. And it was so stupid, so unnecessary.

Anton didn't switch off the engine when he pulled up outside her shop. On the other hand he made no move to get out of the car either.

'Anton, please . . .' She was determined to shatter this tension, to make him see that there was no reason for it to be like this. '. . . I don't want it to end like this. I don't want it to end at all. I love you.'

He smiled thinly. 'I know.' But she didn't love him enough. Maybe she would realise that for herself in time. It was not for him to point it out to her. That wouldn't do her any good. She had come a long, long way over the past five months, but she still had some growing to do, a few things to learn. And he had already done as much as he could.

'Come in with me,' she was saying. 'Stay the night. Please, Anton! There's no reason why we shouldn't continue as we are. We don't need marriage. What's wrong with things as they are, now that——'

She stopped abruptly at the look on his face. He was smiling in such a way that she was forced to acknowledge that they were, once again, worlds apart. But this time it was in their thinking.

'It isn't enough, Lorna. My darling girl, you just don't understand, do you? I don't want you just to share my bed. I want you to share my *life*. I want you to travel with me, live with me, worry with me, laugh with me. I want it permanently, Lorna, not just in brief snatches. I want something you are far from ready to give—commitment. Maybe you'll never be ready, or able, to commit yourself to a man. But for me, nothing less will do. Not now. I love you too much to settle for less. This is goodbye, Lorna. It has to be. I can't handle things any other way.'

He got out of the car and opened the door for her, a gentleman to the last. He even saw her safely inside the shop. And all the time, Lorna was telling herself she would get over him soon enough. She was telling herself it was better to make a clean break, after all. For him and for her.

'Goodbye, Lorna.' He touched her face briefly as he turned to go. 'Take good care of yourself.'

Anton drove home slowly, automatically, without an ounce of concentration. The ring was in his pocket. He had forgotten all about it. He wanted her to have it, as a memento. Maybe he would post it to her.

CHAPTER TWELVE

THE days moved on inexorably. They were long, empty days. After the first week, Lorna thought she was over the worst. The first week without Anton was bound to be the worst, wasn't it?

How could she have allowed herself to get into this position in the first place? Hadn't she once vowed that no man on earth would ever have any kind of influence on her life? And she had stuck to that rigidly ... until Anton.

Falling in love with him had been an insidious process—she had said something similar to Eve when admitting how much she had changed since meeting him. She honestly wished now that she was the person she used to be before last Christmas. Life was safe then. She had had peace, inner peace. Of course, she would have that again. She would get over him soon enough. The first week without him was bound to be the worst.

'Lorna, are you all right?'

Dulcie was calling upstairs to her and it startled her out of her reverie. 'Yes!' She called back firmly, confidently. What was she doing up here anyhow, standing in her flat on a Saturday afternoon?

Her mind was blank, quite blank. She glanced around the room, her expression vacant. Of course! She had come upstairs to make some sandwiches.

May was drawing to a close and Dulcie had been working Saturdays since the start of the month because the student who used to come in had left. The tourist season was well under way, but the weather was foul today and nobody was walking around the town unless they absolutely had to. No one with any sense, at any rate. The rain was bouncing off the ground, rushing along the gutters.

Her other part-time assistant was in the shop, and Lorna had volunteered to make sandwiches so no one would need to go out and buy them in this downpour. And what had she done instead? She had stood by the window in her living room, watching the rain, her thoughts going round in circles. 'This isn't good enough!' She said it aloud as if this would give the words more impact. 'This is pathetic. You are pathetic. If this is what love does to you, you're well out of it.'

Readjusting to her old routine was not easy. She couldn't make herself interested in anything happening around her, and she spent the weekend wondering what she used to do with herself on her days off. Nothing, was the answer to that. But she had been content with it, then.

The second week was no easier. In fact it was worse, in spite of the efforts she made to distract herself, to busy herself. On the Wednesday afternoon she picked up some stock in London and spent the evening marking it up, washing some bedlinen and doing her ironing.

Dulcie had not said a word to her about Anton. Not after she had told her, shortly and simply, that she wouldn't be seeing him again. Lorna was grateful that for once Dulcie had asked no questions, but her curiosity was almost tangible. In fact at times it looked more like concern—which was quite unnecessary.

'Lorna, did you pick these up yesterday?' Dulcie looked through the new dresses and blouses on the following morning. 'Are you sure these prices are right? Or is there some reason they're to be sold so cheaply?'

Irritated, Lorna looked into it. She hadn't put on any profit at all. She had put them on sale at the price she had paid for them—excluding the VAT.

Dulcie tried to laugh it off, but there was no mistaking it now, she was concerned about Lorna, and it irritated her beyond words. Oh, she wasn't irritated with her assistant, she was irritated with herself. She was not in command. And it wasn't the first time she'd made stupid mistakes—in the shop and when doing her books. 'Here are the invoices, Dulcie. Put new price tags on—mark them up as usual, will you? I—I'm going out for a couple of hours.'

She shouldn't have gone out, not on a Thursday when Dulcie would be left on her own. But she had to; the shop seemed claustrophobic all of a sudden.

Eve came on the following Sunday. She had been on honeymoon for a month, but she was bound to come visiting sooner or later.

'You look great! Look at that suntan!' Lorna greeted her cheerfully, determined to be her usual self. 'Have you had a good time, or is that a silly question?'

Eve spoke enthusiastically about the Caribbean—enthusiastically and very briefly. She quickly got down to the real reason for her visit. 'We got back yesterday evening and we called at Anton's on the way from the airport. We thought we'd—we'd surprise you. *Both* of you. You can imagine the shock I got on hearing what had happened! Lorna——'

Lorna was filling the kettle, not looking at her.

'Please don't bother with tea. I can't stay—I'm back in the office tomorrow and I've got loads to do at home. Let's sit down. Tell me what it's all about.'

Eve was very upset, that much was obvious. That she should demand to know all the details was unlike her. She never pried. She deserved some kind of explanation.

Lorna sat down, but as soon as she opened her mouth to speak, she burst into tears. Great heaving sobs shook her body and she just couldn't seem to stop them. Mortified, Eve shot to her side and held her tightly, as a mother might hold a child, comforting and almost crying with her.

It was a long time before Lorna got a grip on herself. When she was finally able to speak, she found herself telling the whole story. She told her friend everything, absolutely everything, not only about her relationship with Anton, about their previous meeting last October and the reason for it, but also about Jake Dougan and her history prior to him and after him.

Eve was with her for hours, and when Julian telephoned to ask when she was going home she fobbed him off and told him to get his own dinner. She listened intently to Lorna, asking the occasional question, encouraging her to go on.

As a solicitor Eve was not easily surprised by the things people told her. She had handled many a case in which she had heard worse stories. 'I can't tell you how much I appreciate your trust, Lorna. You've always been a mystery to me, you know. But I understand you now—I understand everything.'

'Everything?' Lorna looked up in disbelief. 'My reasons for not wanting to marry Anton?'

'Yes,' Eve sighed, 'those, too. Dear lord, it took me long enough to get round to marriage. But when you meet the right man . . .' She paused, her eyes examining Lorna's face. 'I—I thought that he . . . Well, to be truthful I thought from the beginning that Anton was right for you. Of course I had no idea about your meeting before Christmas. I mean, so much falls into place now. But even so—Lorna, I *still* think he's the right man. Look how you've changed. From someone who wouldn't glance twice at a man to—to this! You are in love with him, you can't deny it.'

'I am! I've told you that. But I haven't changed sufficiently that I can hand myself over into someone else's care. *Anyone* else's. Even Anton's. I've been my own boss for a long time. I like my freedom. I need my independence. I can rely on myself without fear of being let down! Don't you see? Do you see it, Eve?'

'Yes,' Eve said simply, honestly. She did understand, all of it. It was easy to see how Lorna's mind worked, but the top and bottom of it was that she didn't love Anton enough. Anton had, in fact, told Eve and Julian that. And he was right. There was really no more to be said. 'Darling, I really must go now. I want you to pick up that phone and come round to us any time you like, okay? Don't be on your own if you don't want to be.'

'I'm sorry to have burdened you with all this, especially when you've just got home. But thank you for listening. You've been a help. You're good friends, you and Julian. You and your husband.' Lorna smiled. 'You can tell him if you like. Tell Julian as much as you want.'

'Perhaps,' Eve shrugged. 'Maybe I'll tell him the basics. If I do it will go no further, you know that.'

Lorna nodded. There had been a time when she would tell nothing about herself to anyone. And the result of that had been that nobody understood her but Cathy. While she still would never talk to people in general, would never talk idly about herself, at least she had started to trust a special few. That was just one of the changes she had gone through since meeting Anton . . .

Eve was lingering, seeming suddenly uncomfortable. 'What is it?' asked Lorna. 'Say it, Eve, it's all right.'

'No, I—I don't want to say anything. It's just . . .' Eve opened her handbag and pulled out a small velvet box. 'Anton asked me to give you this. He wants you to keep it, Lorna—he made that quite clear. He said it will go with your pearls.'

Lorna took the box and opened it, almost dreading to look because she knew what was inside it. She snapped it shut again. 'It's . . . an engagement ring.' She thrust it into Eve's hand. 'Wait a minute.'

In her bedroom were the pearls he had given her for her birthday. She had put them back in their box on the night they had said goodbye, sealed it in an envelope on which she had written his address. Now, she handed it to Eve. 'The pearls. I can't keep them, Eve, any more than I could accept that ring. Give them back to him for me.'

'I think you're making a mistake. He really wants you to keep——'

'I *can't*. Please do this. I'm sorry to involve you like this, but please do it. I was too nervous to post them, I didn't dare send them with a taxi driver. Well, I just didn't want to take a risk . . .'

Eve put the boxes in her bag. 'I understand.'

'Look, I'm sorry to use you like this when you're caught in the middle——'

'Stop apologising!' With a brief hug and a reminder to go round for dinner any time, Eve left.

No sooner had Lorna got back upstairs than she started crying again. The ring! The ring had been exquisite, a beautiful pearl which matched perfectly the necklace Anton had given to her. It was nestling in a delicate setting on a band of platinum.

She was crying silently now, filled with an unaccountable pain the like of which she had never before experienced. How thoughtful he was! How like him that was! He must have chosen it when he bought the necklace, he must have planned then that he would give her the matching ring on the day he asked her to marry him, on the day he took her to his house—the home he had created for them.

Lorna had thought she was well aware of Anton's qualities, but it was only during the following days that she acknowledged fully the extent of them, that she acknowledged the extent to which he loved her. The more she remembered, the more she realised just how much that was.

There was a time during the following week when she simply walked out of the shop in the middle of the morning and left her staff to cope. She drove for miles, giving no thought to distance or time.

'You're only half alive,' Cathy had once said to her. Dear God, she was fully alive now! The pain inside her was there to confirm it. And it wouldn't go away. It just continued to get worse.

Until she had seen that ring and realised what it represented, she had not stopped to think about how Anton was feeling. How was he feeling now? What kind of fool was she, that she could turn down a love like that? She had never been loved in her life, and when love had finally come to her, it had come in such abundance. How precious it was! And she had in effect rejected it.

What she had done to deserve such love, she couldn't imagine. What had she ever given to Anton? Ever? Nothing but test after test after test. She hadn't realised that this was what she had been doing, but she saw now that it was so. She had been waiting for him to let her down in some way. But he never had. Why had she been convinced that he would? Because she hadn't realised how deeply he loved her, that was why. Also because her past, her general past, was *still* influencing her.

Nothing in her life had been constant until she had opened *Feline*, and she couldn't believe that anything in her future would be constant—nothing which involved men, anyhow. And certainly not marriage.

As for *Feline* . . . How did she feel about her precious business now? She couldn't care less about it. She could think of nothing but Anton.

She started the car. She had parked in a layby, too distressed to drive any further. She did not go to Anton then. It was one morning in early July when she did that.

The sun was streaming through the curtains and Lorna woke up with the strangest feeling, a feeling of complete and utter calm. It was unlike anything she had experienced before. In the past she had known peace, but it had been false, unreal, just the obvious result of shutting herself off from life. She realised that it had not in fact been peace but rather a lack of disturbance because she was, emotionally, dead.

It had been over six weeks since she had seen Anton. Six weeks of emptiness, not only in her life but in her heart. That and the pain she had been living with. Dear lord, how she had missed him! Yet it had all been worthwhile. She had spent six weeks in a kind of . . . a kind of vacuum, but she had learned a great deal in that time. She had learned for one thing that love was giving, thinking of the loved one before thinking of oneself. As Anton had.

She got out of bed and bathed. She dressed and put

on her make-up as she had done every morning ...
until a few weeks ago. Recently she had neglected her
appearance because she no longer cared about her
image as the owner of *Feline*. Image? She didn't have an
image now. She was someone else. She was *herself*, and
that was someone new.

This morning she was going to see Anton and she
wanted to look her best for him. For him, and nothing
and nobody else. In future that was how it would be.
She wanted to please him, to make him happy. She was
going to be the best wife in the world.

It was no longer strange to her, the feeling of
complete and utter calm with which she had woken up.
It was born of the knowledge that she was loved
absolutely, totally. That knowledge brought confidence
in its wake, the confidence to strip away her final
emotional barrier.

Lorna stood calmly by the door of the shop,
waiting for Dulcie's arrival. The older woman frowned
as soon as she set eyes on her boss. Lorna was
looking so much better today, but there was something
strange about her. 'What is it, Lorna? Are you going
out again for the day? Aren't you going to work
today?'

'I'm going out for good.' She didn't mean to be
cryptic, and she explained herself because she owed it to
Dulcie to do so. 'I'm going to see Anton, so don't look
worried. I'm going out of this shop now, and I'm never
going to work in it again.'

'You're—going to talk to him?' Dulcie's frown
cleared. 'Oh, Lorna, I'm so glad! He loves you so
much!'

'Yes. Quite how much—well, I was the last to
realise.'

'He asked you to marry him, didn't he? Please tell
me. Is that what your fight was about?'

'Yes. You see, Dulcie, I was shocked by that. I'm
really very stupid. I was the last person to realise that,
too—that he would propose. It took me by surprise and

I reacted stupidly because the idea of marriage scared me.'

Dulcie smiled. 'You're not unique. A lot of people feel like that.'

'Perhaps. But it doesn't scare me any longer. I'll take my chances! Anton and I couldn't start with better foundations.' She turned to go, eager to go, but Dulcie called to her.

'Wait a minute!' She waved her arms about helplessly. 'What—what about *Feline*? Are you letting it go?'

'It can rot for all I care. Yes, I'm letting it go. I'm letting go of *everything* in the past, Dulcie. And that includes this shop.' Lorna shrugged apologetically, realising she was being cryptic again. Dulcie must think her quite mad. 'I'm sorry. Manage it for me until I sell it. Buy it yourself. Close it right now—I really don't care.'

She left without another word, seeing the look of surprise on Dulcie's face. But Dulcie was not entirely puzzled, only a little.

Lorna drove unhurriedly to the farmhouse. She wasn't going to risk an accident. She knew exactly what she was doing; she was cool and calm.

Anton's dogs came bounding towards the car and she hesitated momentarily before opening her door. But she needn't have worried. They remembered her all right. She had been there with their master; she could be admitted. Better than that, they greeted her.

And then Mrs Gray was there, trying unsuccessfully to get the dogs under her control. 'Wolf! Leo! Heel!' She looked at Lorna apologetically, obviously pleased to see her. 'Miss Stewart! I'm sorry about these two devils. My husband handles them much better than I can. Oh, it's so nice to see you! I'm so glad——' She broke off.

'What is it?' Fear clutched at Lorna's heart like an icy hand. 'Is something wrong, Mrs Gray? Where's Anton?'

'He's not here, miss.' The housekeeper looked really upset.

'He's not in the barn—his studio, rather?'

'He's in Holland, I'm afraid. He went three days ago. He's gone to attend a funeral.'

'A funeral? It—is it someone in his family? Not his father!'

'No, it's a friend of his father. Someone Mr Anton had known all his life, he said. But——'

'But what?' Lorna wanted to shake the woman. 'But what?'

'Well, it's just that I don't know when he'll be back.' There was sympathy in her eyes now. She felt so sorry for this girl. Almost as sorry as she'd felt for Mr Anton these past weeks. Between moving into the staff cottage and the night when he brought his young lady to see the house, Mr Anton had spoken of her a hundred times. Poor Miss Stewart . . . she had never seen anyone look so disappointed . . . it was showing in her eyes.

Lorna took the news quite well, considering. She was crushed by disappointment. It knocked her sideways for a moment. But it didn't matter. She would simply wait, as Anton had waited for her.

'Mrs Gray, I'm going home now and I'll be back in one hour. I'll be back with as many clothes as I can carry in two suitcases. I'm moving in—I'm moving in until Anton gets back. And when he gets back, I'm going to marry him.' She was talking confidently, leaving no room for possible resistance. 'So you needn't worry about this. I'll take full responsibility.'

Mrs Gray nodded, suppressing a smile. Was Miss Stewart expecting an argument or something? Well, she wouldn't get one! Mrs Gray said nothing at all, except, 'I'll have the kettle on when you arrive.'

'The trouble is, we don't know how to contact him.' Mrs Gray glanced at her husband before looking worriedly at Lorna. They were all in the kitchen, drinking tea. 'He phoned yesterday afternoon, after the funeral I suppose, and he said he was going to stay with a friend for a few days. He said we should expect him when we saw him. Still, I suppose I could ring his father. I've got the number——'

'No,' Lorna said firmly, 'I don't want that. And if he happens to ring again, don't tell him I'm here. I—want to surprise him.' She wanted to see his face, was what she really meant.

Of course Mr and Mrs Gray knew very well what she meant. 'He's been very good to us, you know,' Mr Gray said. 'Did my wife tell you what had happened to us? No? I was made redundant. 'Course, at my age it's not easy finding a job—not when I haven't got any skills. Betty was working as a daily to Mr Anton's cousin——'

'Miss Stewart knows that,' his wife put in. 'I told you that's where I first met her. At Mr Karel's place.'

'Sorry. Yes.'

'Let me tell the story, John.' Mrs Gray took over and explained to Lorna how she had told Anton of her husband's redundancy when he had called in to see Karel some time ago. 'He knew that we lived in a Council house, that it would be a tight squeeze for us to manage with John out of work—and he asked me if we'd like to work for him here. Both of us. And he told me about the cottage—'course, I'm not really a cook——'

'If I could cook as well as you, I'd be very happy. You can teach me a few things.' Lorna meant it, too. The one and only meal she'd had so far from Anton's housekeeper had been very good indeed. Maybe she would never be as good as Eve, but she could certainly manage the basics.

'And with the children long since married, and the chance to live in the country——'

Mr and Mrs Gray rambled on and Lorna was quite happy to let them. She had nothing else to do. She had nothing to do but wait for Anton.

During the next few days she had misgivings only once. It was nothing serious, nothing to do with herself and Anton and their future together. But she did wonder about the 'friend' he was staying with in Holland. Was it a woman? An old flame, perhaps? It didn't worry Lorna, even if this were the case. She was secure in Anton's love and she wasn't anxious about any possible transference of his love to someone else, real or unreal. Nor did she allow herself to become neurotic when she acknowledged that while she was sleeping in his bed, he was possibly sleeping in someone else's. True, she didn't like the idea, but she could hardly blame him if he were. She tended to think this wouldn't be the case . . .

But what if he were with someone he'd had an affair with in the past? Someone very familiar to him, someone who had been a friend as well as a lover? Might he bring her home with him? For a holiday? To show her his house, the sights of the south of England? It was possible. Anton was obviously in need of company at the moment, otherwise he would have come home after the funeral.

It was that, and only that, over which she had misgivings. It would be embarrassing for him, for her, for the woman concerned, if Anton brought her back from Holland for some reason or other.

Apart from that, she was happy while waiting. At night she slept in Anton's bed and entertained herself with the knowledge that he would soon be in it with her. She entertained herself with trivia, too—like wondering which side of the bed he would prefer when he was no longer alone in it. Like wondering whether he used an electric razor or an ordinary one. To think that she had never spent a night with him! It seemed impossible, all things considered. They had shared such intimacy . . . How she wanted him! She wanted to know the fullest extent of his lovemaking. She wanted so much to be one with him. Mentally, physically and spiritually.

The days slipped by—no, they dragged slowly by. But she didn't allow herself to think that he would be away for a long time. She spent her days walking the dogs, reading in his studio in the barn, enjoying the house and the grounds. She shopped for flowers and some houseplants and kept herself generally busy.

Anton came home in the middle of the night. It was the sixth night after Lorna had moved in and because she wasn't expecting him (he had not telephoned at all) she had gone to sleep as usual.

Anton opened the front door and went straight upstairs. He was shattered. It hadn't made much sense really, taking a late flight when he could easily have taken a daytime one. But what did make sense these days? He was by no means himself in so many ways. He'd been glad to get out of this house, though sorry about the circumstances which brought his trip about. But now he was back, he wished he weren't. He had lost interest in the place.

There was plenty of work about for an architect of his calibre. He had taken on a few simple projects and one of them had yet to be finished. Perhaps he would stop refusing work now, now he knew that that was the only thing which might serve to distract him from his thoughts. Yes, he would inundate himself with work. Nothing else had helped him to forget her. Drowning himself in work wouldn't do that, either. But at least it would serve as a distraction.

It happened when he got to the top of the stairs. He stopped dead, sensing that he was not alone. There was someone in the house. He had come straight upstairs, had switched on the hall light, but there was no movement in any of the rooms. His eyes flitted around quickly as he walked towards his bedroom. What the hell was he thinking about? The dogs were outside. They'd come bounding around the house when he'd parked at the front door. Nobody had got past them, that was for certain.

But his hand stopped in mid-air as he reached for the handle of his bedroom door. If there was someone in there, they'd be far sorrier about it than he would.

And then he knew.

He hadn't seen her car, but he knew she was here. He stood perfectly still, resigned to, even mildly amused by, the way his breathing quickened. He made no attempt to control it.

He revelled in it.

She was here, in his bed, and she was waiting for him. For how long had she been waiting for him? Anton opened the door quietly, letting only the landing light into the room. He stood for several seconds looking at the outline of her body in the bed, his bed, their bed. Then he switched on a lamp and stood by her side. Still she didn't wake up. The barking of the dogs, the sound of his car, the lights had not and did not disturb her.

He smiled, unable to take his eyes off her face. To think that he had only seen her sleeping once before—in his car. How beautiful she was! He touched her lightly on the shoulder and her eyes came open instantly.

What was happening to his breathing, his heartbeat, he had no control over. Nor could he prevent the joy he felt on seeing her. But that was as far as it went. Over his mind he had a certain amount of control: he dared not hope for too much until she told him *why* she was here. Was she here to tell him she still wanted him as friend and lover, and nothing else? Or was she here because——

Lorna blinked several times against the light, moving rather dazedly as she started to stretch in the most incredibly provocative manner, the duvet shifting so that her naked breasts were revealed to him. Anton didn't move a muscle until her eyes came open properly, until they met with his and he could see for himself that he had not hoped in vain. It was there, in her eyes, that which he had waited so long to see!

Those eyes! They had always spoken for her, always told him what she was feeling. During the time he had known her he had seen so many emotions reflected in those big, beautiful green eyes of hers—anger, fear, worry, love. Love. Yes, he had seen that before, but not to this degree! He had never seen anything like this!

He sat on the bed, reaching for her as she reached for him. It was a long, long time before he spoke, before he could find his voice.

Perhaps that was just as well. Lorna was babbling excitedly, as if she had just discovered an entirely new continent. Perhaps she had. Anton had had to make allowances for the fact that she had never known profound love, protective love, of any description—parental love, the love of an old friend. There had only been Cathy who had ever cared anything about her. She had certainly not known the love of one man for one woman. Maybe that was why she had been so slow to recognise it when it came to her. For that reason and for many more.

'Anton! Anton, I've been so stupid—so very stupid, my darling. Can you forgive me? I didn't realise—I said such silly things to Eve——' She was bubbling over, babbling incoherently. She was aware of it and she couldn't stop herself. There was so much she wanted to say. So much! She had to explain to him, she had to make him see—Oh, God, he was here, home! Alone. He had taken her in his arms and was still being patient with her, as patient as ever, when she really couldn't be making much sense.

Anton brushed her hair from her forehead, watching the tears gathering in her eyes. 'Hush, darling. Take it easy. I know only too well what you've been through.'

She wriggled away from him, putting both her hands in his. 'No, I must explain. I must! I've been so selfish, Anton. Can you forgive me? These past weeks have been terrible for you, my darling. I know, because that's how it's been for me. But for me—for me it was necessary, you see, because it's brought me to this.'

'This?'

'This realisation of how much I love you.' She searched his eyes anxiously. 'I've thought about nothing but you. And the more I thought, the more I loved you. I told Eve that I wouldn't marry you because I liked my freedom. I said I needed my independence.' Lorna laughed shortly, shaking her head. 'But these past weeks have shown me I'm not free, not independent.' She moved into his arms and clung to him tightly. 'I belong with you now. I belong with you.'

He just held her against him, stroking her hair, content to let her pour it all out. She loved him enough, and that was all that really mattered. Maybe she had loved him enough all along, maybe she had just been afraid of admitting it to herself.

'And do you know what else I said to Eve? I said I could rely on myself without fear of being let down. What *rubbish*! I came close to ruining my own life! I don't know how I've lived without you all this time. But I was afraid, you see, afraid of putting my happiness, my future, into someone else's hands.' She moved away slightly so she might see his eyes, watching him smile that very special smile of his. 'But it's a two-way commitment, isn't it, Anton? You would be doing exactly the same thing.'

'Indeed I will.' He pulled her against him, brushing his lips very lightly over hers, the way she once did to him when she first kissed him . . . a hundred years ago.

'I'm yours,' she murmured against his lips. 'Body and soul.'

He quirked an eyebrow at her. The anxiety had gone from her eyes, but he wanted to see her smiling again, laughing again. 'What were you saying about body and soul . . .?'

She laughed at his roguish grin, then she shrugged helplessly. 'But darling, you must be tired after your journey . . .'

Anton got to his feet and took his jacket off, keeping his back to her. 'Yes, I am rather.'

'Hey!' she squealed. 'You weren't supposed to say that! Anton? Anton!'

He laughed inwardly at her note of indignation, keeping his face straight as he turned to look at her. She was standing by the bed now, naked and perfectly beautiful in the soft glow from the lamp. His pulses were throbbing with desire, his eyes trailing over every inch of her as she walked slowly towards him. He shoved his hands into his pockets and tore his eyes away, fixing them on an invisible spot on the wall. 'It's no good, Lorna. There's nothing you can do to revive me.'

'Is that so?' She slipped her hands under his sweater, pulling herself tightly against his body. 'Something tells me you're lying,' she whispered. 'So it's no use playing hard to get.'

Best Seller Romances

These best loved romances are back

Mills & Boon Best Seller Romances are the love stories that have proved particularly popular with our readers. These are the titles to look out for this month.

UNWANTED BRIDE Anne Hampson
NIGHT OF THE YELLOW MOON Flora Kidd
HAWK IN A BLUE SKY Charlotte Lamb
THE WRONG MAN TO LOVE Roberta Leigh
LORD OF LA PAMPA Kay Thorpe
THE LOVED AND THE FEARED Violet Winspear

Mills & Boon

the rose of romance

ROMANCE

Variety is the
spice of romance

Each month, Mills & Boon publish new
romances. New stories about people falling in
love. A world of variety in romance — from the
best writers in the romantic world. Choose from
these titles in November.

CHAINS OF REGRET Margaret Pargeter
BELOVED STRANGER Elizabeth Oldfield
SUBTLE REVENGE Carole Mortimer
MARRIAGE UNDER FIRE Daphne Clair
A BAD ENEMY Sara Craven
SAVAGE ATONEMENT Penny Jordan
A SECRET INTIMACY Charlotte Lamb
GENTLE PERSUASION Claudia Jameson
THE FACE OF THE STRANGER Angela Carson
THE TYZAK INHERITANCE Nicola West
TETHERED LIBERTY Jessica Steele
NO OTHER CHANCE Avery Thorne

On sale where you buy paperbacks. If you
require further information or have any difficulty
obtaining them, write to: Mills & Boon Reader
Service, PO Box 236, Thornton Road, Croydon,
Surrey CR9 3RU, England.

Mills & Boon
the rose of romance

How to join in a whole new world of romance

It's very easy to subscribe to the Mills & Boon Reader Service. As a regular reader, you can enjoy a whole range of special benefits. Bargain offers. Big cash savings. Your own free Reader Service newsletter, packed with knitting patterns, recipes, competitions, and exclusive book offers.

We send you the very latest titles each month, postage and packing free – no hidden extra charges. There's absolutely no commitment – you receive books for only as long as you want.

We'll send you details. Simply send the coupon – or drop us a line for details about the Mills & Boon Reader Service Subscription Scheme.
Post to: Mills & Boon Reader Service, P.O. Box 236, Thornton Road, Croydon, Surrey CR9 3RU, England.
*Please note: READERS IN SOUTH AFRICA please write to: Mills & Boon Reader Service of Southern Africa, Private Bag X3010, Randburg 2125, S. Africa.

Please send me details of the Mills & Boon Subscription Scheme.
NAME (Mrs/Miss) _____ EP3
ADDRESS _____

COUNTY/COUNTRY _____ POST/ZIP CODE _____
BLOCK LETTERS, PLEASE

Mills & Boon
the rose of romance